The Promise
Fulfilled

The Promise Fulfilled

Tomorrow's Medicine Today

Michael P. Wicks

Printed in Canada
First printing November 2002
Book Jacket & Page Layout Design by:
LB Graphics
lilo@lbgraphics.ca
ISBN: 0-9725196-0-2

For more information on the QXCI
please contact
Quantum Life L.L.C.
Tel: 1 (866) 869-0278
email: info@quantum-life.com
www.quantum-life.com

About the Author

Michael Wicks lives in Victoria, British Columbia with his wife and two teenage sons. He is the president of Your Corporate Writer, a company that offers a wide range of professional writing services to the business, corporate and non-profit sectors. His career in publishing has taken him all over the world and his love for books and the written word borders on obsession. Just picking up a pristine new book by a favorite author can bring tears to his eyes. Like the hero of The Promise Fulfilled, he is always searching for the meaning of life, the universe and everything – and it isn't 42.

Author's Note

Dear Reader

You are about to embark on a journey of discovery into the world of a medical device called the Quantum Xrroid Conscious Interface (QXCI) and discover tomorrow's medicine today. It will change the way you look at the healthcare industry forever and help you realize that you are more in control of your health than you could ever have imagined.

Although written as a novel, the book is actually 'faction' a cross between fiction and non-fiction. Most of the characters really exist, some even keep their real names and lead their own lives, others have had their character manipulated a little to make the story flow. One such character is Simon (who bears a striking resemblance to me) whose story and personality have been adapted somewhat to help the storyline.

All practitioners and patients using the QXCI are real people. However, I have changed their names and even gender, relocated them to other cities, towns and even changed their nationality to protect their privacy.

Some of the events in their case studies have been altered, once again to protect their privacy, but their relationship with the QXCI, their medical concerns and the results they experienced, are just as they were related to my researcher or me.

The most important thing to note is that when you are reading about the QXCI, the practitioners that use it and the patients that have benefited from it, you are reading their true story.

As they say in the movies 'although based on a true story, certain events in this book have been fictionalized for dramatic effect'.

For
Sheila, Adam and Joshua
and the QXCI team - Bill, Karen and Ryan

C O N T E N T S

Prologue 1

Quantum Coincidence 7

The Journey Begins 17

Taking Control 41

Budapest 45

The QXCI Experienced 65

The Nelson Principles of Healing 79

A Wake-Up Call 111

The QXCI Explained 115

QXCI: Another Way 153

Hannah's Epiphany 159

The Promise Fulfilled 203

PROLOGUE

After a doctors' strike in Israel where several hundred thousand appointments and tens of thousands of surgeries were cancelled, a study showed that there was a 40% decrease in deaths during the period of the strike. A similar reduction was observed in 1983 when doctor's also went on strike [1].

I have always thought of myself as an agnostic; you know, someone who believes that human knowledge is limited to experience. It's not that I haven't wanted to believe; I've sat in churches longing for God to talk to me often enough. But the leap of faith required to believe, without tangible evidence, has always proved totally elusive to me. Of course, I have considered just believing; you know, faking it. After all, then I could pray and go to church and receive all the other benefits faith brings. The trouble is, I would always know that it was all a lie and I've never been big on having hypocrisy as a bedfellow.

So, when I met Karen and Ryan my guard was up and my antennae receptive to the possibility of worshipping false gods, or in this case false technology and even worse, rampant idealism. As it turns out I needn't have worried.

---

[1] British Medical Journal June 2000; 320: 1561

This is the story of a personal journey of belief, growth and realization that started in all innocence at a Starbucks coffee shop on the West Coast of Canada; took me to Eastern Europe (Budapest to be precise), and ended up changing the way I thought about myself and medicine forever. More importantly, it led me to believe in something that was, to all intent and purpose, 'Star Trek' medicine. I remember a machine that featured in early episodes of that classic television series, where intergalactic crew members were hooked up to a highly sophisticated device that provided a detailed assessment of their health status. It then miraculously set about identifying causes, providing remedies and balancing their body functions like a graphic equalizer crazily reading the Rolling Stones classic Jumping Jack Flash. I remember thinking all those years ago what a different world it would be if a medical device like that really existed and how much suffering could be alleviated. Little did I know then that someday I would discover such a machine, and even more astounding, that when I did powerful people would feel threatened by it and try to dismiss its existence, even try to denigrate its potential.

We will explore the mysterious and mind-blowing universe of quantum physics, quantum biology and energetic medicine, the world of Stephen Hawkin, Professor William (Bill) Nelson and an advanced treatise on subspace, and the quantum aspects of biology called 'Promorpheus'. It is a world where a machine can assess a person's total health status in a matter of minutes and where major illnesses and diseases can be treated in non-invasive ways without using synthetic drugs. This is the same world where the synthetic drug industry is worth billions of dollars annually, and where highly intelligent men and women who practice alternative medicine are targets solely because they pose a threat.

Perhaps I should introduce myself: my name is Simon. I am an Englishman, now a Canadian citizen, living on the West Coast of Canada. I escaped an increasingly stressful life in an over-populated and class-driven England some years ago; an England where people drive along country lanes and around blind bends at speeds reserved for four lane highways here on Vancouver Island. I am in my early fifties, married, with two wonderful sons. I like to think I look at least half a dozen years younger than the photo in my passport. I have a mental age of approximately 35 years. If I could have remained any age I wanted, it would have been 35. It was then that I felt that I had achieved full maturity, that at last I was in control of myself and my life. I was young enough and ambitious enough to make a long-term commitment to a company, and old enough to appear to be a safe bet. I enjoyed that year, fleeting though it was, and have always felt that it's been downhill ever since.

I still have my hair and, although encroaching, the grey is limited to a few flecks here and there. I plan to dye it when it transgresses from being distinguished to making me look my age. I never want to look, or act, my age; to do so admits that youth's belief in immortality was just another lie. Although I am fit for my age many people who know me think I have abused my body with excessive alcohol and insufficient exercise, not to mention the three packs of cigarettes a day I smoked until I was thirty. To those people, and they know who they are, I give a symbolic shoulder shrug. I have strong genes and my doctor tells me I should live a long life; although he has some concerns that I appear to be addicted to my own adrenaline. He tells me that if I ever stop to catch a breath in this mad rush called life, I could be in serious trouble. That's okay, I have no plans to slow down - survival is a serious business and there are so many fine wines I have yet to taste.

I am not an academic, but could have been and would have been given the right circumstances. During my early career, I rose from being a query clerk (I've heard all the jokes) for an academic book publisher to a salesman selling books with salacious titles such as My Carnal Confessions, My Bed Is Not For Sleeping and Every Good Boy Deserves a Favour. In spite of this shaky start, I managed to fight my way out of pulp fiction and into the heady world of middle then senior management until I eventually became Managing Director of a small international publishing house. This allowed me to travel the world and finally get, at least in part, the education I felt I deserved. There really is something called the university of life; the syllabus is highly flexible and irregular, but if you work hard, survive the tests and learn from your mistakes, the degree is worth more than academic accreditation.

Later in life I operated my own small businesses in corporate sponsorship and management consulting. But eventually decided, not long ago, to return to my publishing roots and concentrate on being a writer full time.

The outside world sees a lively, charming, fun-loving, workaholic extrovert, but I consider myself a 'feet placed firmly on the ground' person. When it comes to anything that isn't mainstream, my conservatism comes firmly to the forefront. I need things proved to me before believing them and until recently I thought alternative medicine went hand in hand with beads and seeds and marijuana pipes.

Meeting Karen and Ryan was the catalyst for a major change in the way I looked at the medical system, at myself and the world around me. Who says an old fart can't learn new tricks? I found myself answering some long overdue questions about my life, and in the process investigating whether a promise made by a German pioneer named Dr. Voll, working in the field of energetic medicine some seventy years ago would be fulfilled by an eccentric American genius living in an ancient apartment block in Budapest.

QUANTUM COINCIDENCE

My name is Penny, I am a QXCI practitioner. This is my story.

The London Underground was busy, hot and humid; its unique smell of dust, grease and electric contact permeated my clothes in the way only the Northern Line can do. I had arrived in London a few days ago from Canada, my senses heightened by the long absence. Up and down the platform people actively avoided eye contact. They looked at their shoes, and at advertisements for Brooks Brothers promising temporary employment. It was late and there was an increased sense of wariness. People were spaced along the platform as if planted there by some horticulturalist, each given just enough space to survive and flourish. Trains are less frequent at this time of night and hundreds of feet below ground late revelers burrow and wait.

Someone approached me and I felt my guard go up, that survival instinct that puts us on alert when we are unsure whether someone is friend or foe. In this case long before the person entered my personal space, greater at this time of night and in this locale, a sense of familiarity crept over me and encouraged me to make eye contact. It was Sue, a friend I had not seen for some years, an unlikely underground traveller even though a long-term resident of West Finchley, just a few stops north. She must have had that same second sense because she looked up and saw me watching her walk along the platform, her heels clicking on the tile like some tired and rhythm-less tap dancer. Recognition took a few seconds, but the wait was rewarded by a broad smile that crossed the distance of time since we last met.

The last time I had seen Sue she was suffering from chronic fatigue syndrome, an illness so debilitating she couldn't leave her house. But here she was looking great, full of energy, a different woman. A dull roar from the tunnel at the far end of the platform announced the imminent arrival of a train. Seconds later concentrated subway stench was forced from the tunnel as the train chased it out bellowing and clattering. People moved forward in a welcoming ritual. Without thinking Sue and I moved closer to the platform edge readying ourselves for when the doors opened and this metal tube welcomed us in. We talked for a while about how she had overcome her illness and about a device called the QXCI. I listened intently as we travelled north through Camden Town, Kentish Town and Tuffnel Park. Goosebumps formed along my arms and spine as she told me how this device cured her when nothing else could.

Sitting here in my practice on Canada's West Coast I can look back on that simple journey, on what many people call the 'misery line', and know that it changed my life and the way I approach healing. My name is Penny and I graduated from Chinese medical school in the late 1980s in the days when you could still get closed down for practicing medicine without a license and when things like yoga and acupuncture were often called the devil's work. After hearing Sue's story I had to find out more about the device that had cured her. She gave me a contact name and number and within a few months I was the proud owner of my very own Quantum Xrroid Conscious Interface.

When I first started using the device I was one of an elite few and had the wonderful opportunity of training with the master and QXCI creator Dr. Nelson. Learning how to use the device was tough: the computer program that translates the information gathered by the device itself is so incredibly complex I doubt anyone could ever understand or use it to its fullest capacity.

I called as many practitioners that were using it as I could and gathered as much information as possible. I then practiced on any of my friends who were willing to be guinea pigs.

That was five years ago and using the device has been the most wonderful thing I've done in my healing life; not a day goes by that I'm not grateful for having it. It hasn't all been easy though: many people are not ready for such a paradigm shift in the way we diagnose and treat illness. But its time has come. People will have to take notice because its effect is so great that even the pharmaceutical giants may have to bow to its greatness.

A delightful young woman named Hannah called me recently to ask me some questions about the QXCI; apparently some guy is writing a book on the device and she is helping him with the research. She asked me why the device was so special. What a question! I could have answered it in a hundred different ways, but in the end I said 'because it was created by a big mind'.

Most people in the healing professions tend to operate in a niche; we all tend to be specialists of one sort or another. That worries me, as it means no one really has a complete view of the patient. The QXCI provides a truly holistic perspective, one that isn't, in fact can't be, tempered or clouded by bias. After you have used it for a while your personal prejudices disappear and you open up to the many different ways of looking at the human body. The QXCI lets you get inside the body. I have a book called The Household Physician by J. McGregor-Robertson which was published in 1907. It has the most wonderful engravings and a dissection of the human body whereby one can lift flaps to expose the lungs and then these lift up to show the heart, kidneys and liver etc. The QXCI is similar in that it lets me discover what is happening inside the body layer by layer; the power is quite scary sometimes.

I agreed to meet Hannah and discuss some of my experiences with the QXCI. We met in a West Coast restaurant called Rebecca's. Hannah had already arrived and occupied a seat overlooking the harbor where floatplanes jostled with fishing boats and luxury yachts while seagulls squawked and dived above nervous tourists. The mountains in the distance looked as if some giant had dusted them with icing sugar and tiny harbor ferries darted back and forth giving the view a picture postcard perspective.

I warmed to Hannah immediately. Her smile was warm and her eyes intelligent; her handshake, when she rose to greet me, was firm. My earlier reticence about answering questions started to lift.

Her first question was surprisingly probing and centered on how much the success of the QXCI relied on the practitioner's skill and knowledge. I explained that the device was so exceptionally powerful that during a two-hour session the amount of information gathered was more than anyone could ever hope to explain to a patient. Having an understanding of the human body and of diseases is important, I told her, but the device does have the capability of diagnosing and treating patients automatically. Practitioners with experience in alternative healing however, have the ability to maximize the many different programs the device offers.

Hannah noted this down in her reporter's notebook, nodding slowly as if confirming something she already knew.

Our appetizers came and we suspended business talk while we concentrated on our food. Hannah's crab cakes looked appetizing and my steaming spring rolls and radicchio salad was a delightful mix of Asian and West Coast cuisine. I asked about the project and who she was working for. She told me about Simon and how she had met him at a business seminar. She had struck up a business relationship with him, doing some writing and research on an as required basis. We chatted for a while about the food and the restaurant and how lucky we were to live in such a wonderful place until, pleasantries over, she asked me the question most people eventually ask: have you had any big success stories? I suppose everyone is looking for the miracle, the one unexplainable event that proves the device is something out of this world, extraordinary, omnipotent. I could see it was time to bring out the hemorrhoid story.

Ah, the hemorrhoid story! I told Hannah that a few weeks ago a regular patient of mine came to see me for a treatment for shoulder pain. I had been treating the shoulder for a few weeks and it was going well. On this occasion I could see that she was uncomfortable and obviously in pain and when I commented on this she told me that her hemorrhoids were really bad. As we were in the middle of treating the shoulder there was no time to focus on her more personal problem. It surprised me therefore when she called me the following day to thank me for curing her hemorrhoids. Hannah looked confused. I explained: the amazing thing is that the QXCI treats patients in such a holistic way that it harmonizes their entire system, sometimes with surprising results.

Hannah was intrigued by my story but it didn't seem to put her off from finishing her crab cakes and launching into a steaming dish of Aubergine Parmigiana. My Caesar salad was demanding my attention when she asked for another story.

I decided to tell her about Brent, a ten-year-old boy who was brought to me by his mother as a last resort. This child alternated between extreme lethargy and bouts of bad temper, the symptoms of ADD or Attention Deficit Disorder. Ritalin had been suggested as the drug of choice, but the mother had read about the side effects which she recited from memory: disruption of the production of growth hormones, reduced appetite, headache, jittery feelings, gastrointestinal upset, sleep difficulties, irritability, depression, anxiety, blood glucose changes, increased blood pressure, psychosis or paranoia and sometimes permanent changes to the biochemistry of the brain. She wanted to avoid giving this powerful drug to her son if she could. She had a point; I hate to think what she would have said if I had told her that Ritalin comes from the same family as cocaine. In addition the best she could hope for from the drug was that it would treat the symptoms, as it doesn't claim to affect or attack the root cause.

When I tested the child I discovered that he was deficient in dopamine, a chemical messenger that affects a number of brain processes which control movement, emotional response and the ability to experience pleasure and pain. The QXCI chose to feed him dopamine energetically. The next day his mother called to say that the effect was so dramatic it was like having a different son. I treated him for ten days and then he returned for a booster. The length of time between boosters has increased each time and he now only comes for a check-up every couple of months.

I could tell Hannah was captivated by this story, and she told me that she was amazed at the sheer power and potential of this device. She then asked if she could meet a patient and get a first hand account. I told her that I would talk to a few patients and see if any of them would speak to her. She asked if she could have a session on the device herself. In answer to my questioning and suspiciously raised eyebrow, she assured me that she was not out to test the device but to experience it with an open mind. She also mentioned that she had several health issues that she wanted to deal with.

As the meal came to its natural conclusion over coffee she asked me if using the device had any downsides. I told her that there are many issues which can be problematical when using the device, some of them relating to how patients react to dealing with their health problems, others to do more with the practitioner's level of experience. I knew that I wasn't going to be the only practitioner Hannah would talk to so I decided to tell her about one aspect that I felt she would be able to relate to at this stage of her research.

I explained that the machine tests energetically. Through the computer program it has to find the right words to transfer complex energy readings into something the practitioner can understand and relate to the patient. This limited vocabulary means that it may indicate say, lung cancer when in fact it may only mean that there is something in the lungs that has the potential to become cancerous. This is why we always work with the traditional or conventional health system to get things checked through X-Rays, CT or MRI.

Hannah took copious notes and while we waited for the check we talked about the next steps in her research. She said that she would follow up any leads that I could give her and that she was going to contact other QXCI practitioners and patients around the world.

I said goodbye to her outside the restaurant and walked across to the harbor front. Sitting on a bench looking out at the blue waters of the harbor and the mountains in the background I found myself a little envious of the journey Hannah was about to undertake. My journey with the QXCI was a personal one limited to the experiences I'd had and would continue to have with my own patients. Hannah was about to see the wonder of the machine through the unique perspective of many practitioners: naturopaths, chiropractors, reflexologists and traditional medical doctors. Even more, she was going to discover patients whose lives had been changed forever by a mathematician from Ohio living quietly in Budapest.

THE JOURNEY BEGINS

I t was a sunny day in January 2001, when I walked into my local coffee shop to feed my addiction for café lattés. With my coffee, hot, steaming and sprinkled deliciously with shaved chocolate in front of me, I took out my note pad. This is my way of hiding the fact that I am an inveterate people-watcher. Eavesdropping on other people's conversations is a great pastime and for a writer provides wonderful material. At the next table a British accent immediately took my attention - London definitely. A bright, attractive, cheerful and incredibly enthusiastic couple were talking about their business and I was so captivated by them that I blew my cover of pretending to be absorbed in writing in my notebook. The woman smiled at me and by way of admitting I had been listening to their conversation, I asked whether she was English. Totally stupid of course as her accent was most definitely genuine, the real McCoy, but it broke the ice. "Yeh, how'dya guess?" she laughed.

My first impressions were borne out as they told me all about their business in an almost unnervingly frank way. Passion lit their eyes as they discussed how they improved people's health with a mysterious machine called the QXCI. I am always attracted to people with passion and positive attitudes and just knew I had to get to know them better. I had no idea how much my life would become intertwined with theirs, how their past would influence my future and how their future would become part of my story. Unbeknownst to me, a symbiotic relationship was being established which would have repercussions that would echo across generations.

Following my initial lame attempt, I formerly introduced myself to Karen, a petit and beautiful blond with an accent similar to my own southern English inflection, which everyone in North America mistakenly considers Cockney. And then, turning my attention to her partner, I introduced myself to Ryan, a good-looking, young South African. Within minutes it was if we had known each other for years, as if we were just taking over from where we had left off at some other time, some other place. My new friends gushed forth with information about their company, their product and the predicament they were in.

They had come to live in Canada for a while, fallen in love with Victoria and wanted to stay. They needed a business plan to support their application to Immigration Canada for a work permit to allow them to research the potential of relocating their company to the West Coast of Canada. Their product was a state-of-the-art biofeedback machine manufactured in Budapest, Hungary by Karen's ex-husband.

During what turned out to be a tumultuous and chaotic conversation, the sort that so often occurs when ex-patriots meet so far from home, I had mentioned that I was a writer who specialized in writing business plans. When Karen then asked, "Could you write our business plan for us?" it seemed natural to say, "Yes, of course."

I had no idea that my life was about to change irrevocably and that within eight weeks I would fly to Eastern Europe to discuss writing the biography of an eccentric American quantum-physicist living in Budapest. And that from there I would end up writing a book about a truly amazing device, which went by the unlikely name of Quantum Xrroid Conscious Interface, QXCI to its friends.

All this was in the future though and the next few weeks were hectic as the deadline for Karen and Ryan's immigration application drew near and the business plan needed to be written. At their rented house on Saanich Peninsula's beautiful Coles Bay I got to know this fascinating couple and their business, and was drawn into an industry completely foreign to me. During hundreds of hours of conversation and discussion the world of complementary healthcare opened up to me like a tulip in spring, unfolding in answer not only to the questions I needed answering for their business plan, but to my latent concerns about traditional medicine.

I found myself wanting, almost needing, to believe in this mar-velously eccentric, too good to be true, machine. And even though my belief in the efficacy of the machine was already growing, I was still very skeptical about holistic medicine as a concept. I felt that a door had been opened into a whole new world of health and medicine and that once I stepped through, nothing would ever be the same again.

Considering my agnostic attitudes, you may well ask whether I had to make a leap of faith to believe in this machine, this new technology? I would have to answer, 'sort of'. But it happened in stages, as I got to know the host of fascinating characters that make up this story of discovery, and who became such an impor-tant part of my life. You will see for yourself how my transition from skeptic to believer took place, but for now, to give you an idea of how we believe in things we can't yet see or prove incon-trovertibly, I want you to imagine yourself sitting on a bench in the middle of Manhattan, New York. A man runs up to you and tells you that four wild elephants are stampeding down the next street coming your way. Would you believe him? Probably not, but if twenty people, one after another, came running up to you with the same tale you would probably consider joining them in finding a safe spot to watch this extraordinary event. So it was with my experience of complementary medicine and the Disneyesque Quantum Xrroid Conscious Interface device, the story of which unfolds along with my own discovery of self.

A week later I was standing on Karen and Ryan's deck looking out across the dark waters of Coles Bay, while Karen prepared lunch. I started to think about the life I had led for the last fifty plus years. I have never looked after myself particularly well and have often been accused of burning the candle at both ends. Since the age of seventeen I have kept my head down and worked hard, never taking much time off for me, always reaching out for the next dream but never really knowing what it was. Stress becomes a habit, a syndrome which although not a positive force provides a level of comfort by way of familiarity.

The more time I spent with Karen and Ryan the more I realized that there were other less destructive ways of existence. As my gaze drifted toward the funnel end of the bay, I heard the familiar honking of a skein of Canada geese heading my way and recalled the reason why they flew in a 'V' formation. The group all fly in the slipstream shadow of the bird in front, thus preserving their collective energy. The frontrunner, forging ahead with no such protection, is constantly being replaced by another member of the flock. For some reason these new people who had come so unexpectedly into my life were, without knowing it, making me take stock of my life. Suddenly, a whole life trying to be that front bird didn't seem so sensible. Voices drifted back from deep within my memory, "Dad, when are you going to stop

working? You're going to kill yourself. Can't we go out and fly
a kite?" Lost years.

"Simon - lunch!" Ryan's voice pulled me back from my unusual
introspection. Over lunch I learned about allopathic and holistic medicine, the difference between the two and the friction
that clearly exists in two fields which purportedly are fighting for
the same cause - our health and well-being.

Ryan explained that unfortunately traditional medicine (otherwise known as allopathic medicine) has become less about people and more about money. Big business has taken over and with
so many vested interests at stake, politics rather than the
Hippocratic oath seems to be driving it forward as doctors
increasingly become sidelined. Sidelined both by their own professional bodies and by patients who have been conditioned to
believe that they have not received treatment unless they leave
with a prescription for expensive drugs.

As we sat eating the most healthy and organic meal I had experienced for years, Karen carried on from where Ryan had left off,
"Health is a vital component to our happiness." she explained,
"Even though most people live their lives eating junk food,
smoking, drinking alcohol and taking little exercise, they still

expect doctors will just keep putting them right when they go wrong in the same way a mechanic does with a car."

Ryan was nodding enthusiastically, "Our expectation is that doctors are there to fix us, to pass out medications whether we need them or not, to treat the symptoms of our diseases as they occur - to keep us running."

"The crux of it," he continued, "is that we expect our mechanic to fix the root cause of the problem, but when it comes to our health we are often satisfied when our doctor just covers up the symptoms."

We carried on in this vein for some time with Karen and Ryan philosophizing about the weaknesses in approach of traditional medicine and the strengths of a more balanced, multi-disciplinary approach. This made a lot of sense to me and as I mopped up the remaining hummus from my plate with organic pita bread and popped the last Kalamata olive into my mouth, I realized there was an alternative approach to the medical care I was used to, one that focused more on healthcare rather than 'disease-care'. A whole complementary health service that for one reason or another wasn't being made readily accessible to me.

For the rest of the day we worked on the business plan producing a giant 'mind map' that spread like an octopus across four flip-chart sheets of paper spread across their dining room table.

Concentrating on the pragmatic elements of their business halted conversation on the fascinating philosophical differences between traditional and alternative healthcare.

During the drive home I reflected on the discussion at lunchtime and recalled Ryan saying that in reality, there are many answers to the healthcare issues of the world. Some of them undoubtedly lay within the field of traditional medicine, but equally, others are to be found in the field of complementary medicine, especially with devices such as the QXCI. There is a trend toward doctors using complementary medical treatments, especially where there is legislation to ensure full access to complementary health services.

Their comments reminded me that in the past I had often felt like a heretic when complaining about traditional medicine and its blatant inadequacies. It was a surprise to discover that I was not alone.

My reflections during the journey home consisted of more questions than answers and I couldn't help thinking about the few minutes I had spent on their deck overlooking the bay, questioning how stress played such a significant part in my life. I realized I have made an art form of papering over the cracks instead of dealing with issues at the root of my need to be continually moving forward.

I spent the next few days researching the relationship between traditional and alternative medical methodologies and their differing philosophies. Spurred on by my conversations with Karen and Ryan, I had a desire to understand more about why these two factions, with the same goal, could have such different approaches and often be so alienated. I discovered that medical doctors were often harassed by their own governing bodies when practicing complementary medicine. I read about investigators turning up at their offices, carrying out audits and attempting to destroy their practices by publishing reports peppered with falsehoods. In the United States, twelve states have passed legislation allowing doctors to practice complementary medicine without fear from their governing bodies, thirteen more have it on the docket to deal with soon. In Canada, the province of Alberta already has such legislation and in Ontario, where 78% of doctors are already practicing some form of complementary medicine, the provincial government recently passed similar legislation. Reports showed that other provinces across Canada were looking to address this same issue with some urgency.

So, the plot thickened as I found myself in an ideological minefield with the truth entirely dependent on what one believes in, or more importantly, what one doesn't. The issue of faith was rearing its ugly head again.

My agnostic self kept telling me that this could still all be highly dubious fringe medicine that was being promoted by a bunch of wacky weirdoes. On the other hand, my initial investigation into this whole field was showing that traditional medicine didn't have a monopoly on academically superior minds. I was starting to learn about highly intelligent and distinguished scientists, doctors and politicians who not only believed in what this new technology could achieve but also understood how it worked. They were also forthcoming about why significant technological breakthroughs that could alter the way we treat many serious illnesses and diseases, had not been adopted by the traditional medical world in most countries.

A week after my day with Karen and Ryan at their Coles Bay home, I was hiking with my friend, and research assistant, Steve through East Sooke Park. The trail hugs the coastline offering stunning views of the Pacific Ocean and the Olympic mountains; an area so completely West Coast in look and feel, that there isn't anywhere else quite like it in the world. It is a place where Bald eagles soar overhead and build gargantuan nests in Douglas firs that were mere seedlings during the middle ages. A temperate rainforest draped with a moss called Grandfather's Beard, which only grows in areas where the air is completely pure. When I need to think, to get away, there is no better place than this. Oblivious to the stunning beauty and the wonderful ambiance of the place, Gizmo my faithful border collie ran ahead snuffling her way through the undergrowth searching for those smells only animals find appealing. Steve, with his innate ability to know when I need time to think, walked for a long time without saying a word. Our bear bells the only sound to accompany the waves gently brushing the rocks below. In this countryside it is wise to let the wildlife know you are in their territory, as surprising them can lead to unexpected results.

It was in this environment that I found myself trying to rationalize my doubts concerning traditional medicine. From one of those pigeonholes of memory lodged in our brains, I recalled an aunt living in Wales who was let down badly by the medical system. She suffered from a painful and rare medical complaint for fifteen years, a type of eczema of the mouth. Although unsure what it was, doctors treated her symptoms with pastes and creams, steroids and cortisone and even laser surgery, none of which offered anything but minor, temporary relief while at the same time inflicting horrendous side effects. She saw dozens of doctors who concentrated their efforts on treating her symptoms and not the root cause of her illness. Why she was suffering seemed to be of less importance than what new drug, or procedure to try next.

I told Steve the story of my aunt and explained how I felt about a medical system that was designed to focus on dealing with symptoms rather than looking for root causes. Breathing heavily as we climbed the steep slope of a wooded hill, he asked, "What happened to her, did she eventually get cured?"

"What is really amazing", I told him, "is that my aunt didn't seem to want to change what was happening to her. She had been indoctrinated with the belief that anything other than traditional medicine is just so much quackery. The sell job done on this woman was as effective as a cult brainwashing its victims."

Steve grunted and started climbing a particularly steep section of the trail sending a shower of loose rock and gravel down behind him. Reaching some level ground, he turned and said quietly, "A phrase I have often heard at business seminars comes to mind and seems entirely apposite for this situation, 'if you keep on doing the same old things, you will keep on getting the same old results', in this case it appears for fifteen years." Sliding his daypack from his shoulders he sat on the trunk of a recently fallen tree which would eventually become one more nursery log in the evolution of the forest. I could see he was thinking about how to phrase something which meant it was almost certainly going to be one of his sage comments; Steve rarely made off-the-cuff statements.

Gizmo came bounding up thinking that this stop might mean food and Steve reached down to stroke her before saying, "The close-minded attitudes of the traditional medical establishment prevent people such as your aunt from even trying a complementary option. Complementary treatments are rarely recommended by old-school doctors, as their arrogant belief seems to be that 'if I can't cure you no one can' and many patients don't have access to enough information to give them the confidence to try something different. You have to be strong to defy your general practitioner or specialist. People think that if they go to an alternative healthcare practitioner, the doctors and specialists might turn against them and not treat them any more."

He paused and played with Gizmo's ear, then said, "Loyalty based on fear is unhealthy, in more ways than one, but it is an environment that has been cultivated not only in patients but in doctors themselves who are often as frightened of going against the system as are their patients."

Nodding vigorously I said, "I agree Steve, it has been reported that many doctors are frightened of attending complementary health conferences for fear of reprisals from their professional associations and unions. A turf war is on which has little to do with offering effective treatment to patients and everything to do with protecting the self-interests of big business." Steve was nodding enthusiastically so I continued, "The traditional medical industry, and the pharmaceutical companies that support it, just haven't delivered. Medical professionals do their best but have to work within the confines of self-protectionism, either self imposed or externally enforced. If they truly only wanted what was best for their patients, surely they would be open-minded with regard to the thousands of tried and true, ancient and modern alternatives to the narrow-minded focus of traditional medicine."

I looked out to sea and when I turned back Steve was holding his index finger up. "One argument is that complementary medicines have not been tested as stringently as traditional, synthetic drugs," he said.

"There may be some truth in this I agreed. But most of the complementary preparations have been used safely for hundreds of years in dozens of different countries and cultures. On the other hand traditional pharmaceuticals have been responsible for large numbers of illnesses and abnormalities over the years. For all their testing how safe are they?"

"I can see both sides Simon, but I don't have any answers for you."

I respected Steve; his was an old head on young shoulders. His grandfather came to Vancouver Island over sixty years ago from Finland and settled on the West Coast of the island. He built a cabin and then sent for the woman he had married just days before he left Finland to find a new way of life for them both. The cabin was remote, the weather harsh and the life hard, but they raised three children and God was good to them. Steve inherited this steadfastness and stolid approach to life.

Back on the trail we walked in silence for some time, still climbing the hill in zigzag fashion after having to travel inland for several hundred yards to circumnavigate a jagged ravine which cut into the hillside. The surf was loud now as it forced itself into the jagged scar, broke against the rock and shot skyward like some aberrant fountain. As we crested the hill a new sound greeted us, the sound of someone or something struggling in the water. We hurried to the edge to see what the problem was, and looking down at the grey Pacific Ocean we saw a huge Californian sea lion with a huge halibut in its mouth, slamming it against the surface of the water, occasionally diving to eat pieces as the fish broke apart under the thrashing.

Once the show was over my thoughts went back to what Steve and I had been discussing. Too many people refer to anything outside of traditional medicine as 'alternative', which implies 'instead of'. Complementary health practitioners on the other hand see what they do as being inclusive of all other forms of healthcare, working with their traditional medical colleagues, not in isolation to them.

It is true that in many cases our traditional medical doctors do a great job. We go to them and they do their best, based on the level of experience and knowledge they have, to dispense beneficial advice and drugs. But when was the last time you visited a doctor and didn't follow it with a trip to the drug store? A friend recently told me that she had to be adamant about refusing drugs when she went to the doctor. She is not an exception to the rule as more people start to realize that they have other options to ingesting synthetic preparations. Of course, a contrary position exists as patients, inundated with information about how brand name drugs can ease their symptoms and, by inference, solve their problems, request them specifically from their doctors. Perhaps that's the answer, two completely separate healthcare services - traditional and complementary - what a shame it will be if the two can't come together and work for the greater good of the patient.

As we arrived back at our car I commented that we had a lot more research to do. By way of reply Steve grinned, this meant his contract with me would last a little longer, which could only be good news for him. Gizmo jumped into the back of my truck and we headed back to the reality of the city, refreshed.

Our research over the next few weeks came up with some fascinating information. As I read a report from Steve on his findings regarding the pharmaceutical industry, I realized that this project had gone far beyond what was needed for background to a business plan and had become a personal mission.

The Pharmaceutical Industry - An Interim Report: Steve Berg (06/27/00)

The British Medical Journal report, in 1999[2], on the results of a survey of doctors in the United States showed that in 30%-36% of cases doctors gave into requests by their patients to prescribe a specific drug the patient had seen in the media. The worrying fact is that this occurred even when the medicine was not the doctor's first choice for treatment. Patients were basing their decision to request a specific drug primarily on television advertising, followed by television news stories, and then print and other media exposure. In the study, more than half the doctors considered the information provided in the advertisements as only partially accurate. In total, 92% of the doctors in the study felt under some pressure to give patients what they requested.

Given that the pharmaceutical industry spends over $12 billion annually in marketing their drugs and allocates an estimated $8,000 to $13,000 marketing budget per physician in the United States, it is not surprising that there is controversy over the relationship doctors have with drug companies. Physicians have contact with a representative from the pharmaceutical industry on average four times a month. Researchers discovered that there was a correlation between this level of contact and prescribing practices. Also that this resulted in what is described as 'non-rational prescribing' along with preference, and an increase in the prescribing of new drugs with a corresponding drop in generic drugs. The study goes on to report that only 46% of medical students think it unethical to accept gifts (e.g. travel subsidies, training, meals or general gifts) from pharmaceutical companies while 85% think it unethical for politicians to accept gifts of similar type and value.

In a review of the article entitled 'Physicians and the Pharmaceutical Industry - Is a Gift Ever Just a Gift?' published in the Journal of the American Medical Association[3] by Dr. Asley Wazana, from which the information above was obtained, the review concludes that "The present extent of physician-industry interactions appear to affect prescribing and professional behavior and should be addressed at the level of policy and education."

Television commercials for pharmaceutical preparations are prolific. Typically, they portray attractive, happy, smiling and healthy people skipping their way through fields of wild flowers or running along deserted beaches. What could be more natural? Until, the voice-over, in an infuriatingly comforting voice, lists the litany of poten-

---

[3] JAMA.2000;283:373-380. Physicians and the Pharmaceutical Industry; Ashley Wazana, MD, Psychiatry Postgraduate Education, McGill Research and Training Dept.

34

tial side effect: "Some people may experience nausea, dizziness, mood swings etc."

By the way Simon, with regard to the nasal spray for your allergies: you asked me to check it out and I discovered you are exposing yourself to the risk of experiencing the following side-effects: *cataracts, dry mouth, fluid retention, hives, hoarseness, increased pressure within the eye (glaucoma), skin rash, wheezing, cough, headache, light-headedness, nasal burning, nasal and throat dryness and irritation, nausea, nose and throat infections, nosebleed, pain, pinkeye, ringing in the ears, runny nose, sneezing, sore throat, stuffy nose, tearing eyes, unpleasant - or loss of - taste and smell.*

As I sat reading Steve's report it frightened me to think that one drug, a simple hay fever preparation, had the power to potentially affect my body in so many ways.

Simon, these drugs may go through excessive testing but it sure doesn't make them benign. Check this out.

'Can sometimes cause serious side effects. Tardive dyskinesia (a movement disorder) may occur and may not go away after you stop using the medicine.

Signs of tardive dyskinesia include fine, worm-like movements of the tongue, or other uncontrolled movements of the mouth, tongue, cheeks, jaw, or arms and legs. Other serious but rare side effects may also occur. These include severe muscle stiffness, fever, unusual tiredness or weakness, fast heartbeat, difficult breathing, increased sweating, loss of bladder control, and seizures (neuroleptic malignant syndrome).

This is just another regularly prescribed drug - it could even be in your medicine cabinet right now!

I could tell that Steve was in his element and that I would be receiving many more instalments such as this, full of horror stories.

There is a satirical television commercial currently being shown on North American television that shows someone watching a typical pharmaceutical company advertisement. The scene is one of idyllic nature (i.e. fields and beautiful people running along hand in hand, happy to be alive etc.) and then that comforting voice particular to voice-overs starts listing the side effects, including hair loss, deformity and projectile vomiting. At the end of the commercial we return to the person watching the ad who is now sitting at his computer busily selling his pharmaceutical company shares. The advertisement, for an online stockbrokerage service, unwittingly brings home, very succinctly, how insidious pharmaceutical advertising is. It is truly an established and accepted part of our society when it becomes the subject of such obvious satire.

As I considered the implications of all that I had learned over the previous few weeks I realized that the primary difference between traditional and complementary medicine is that the former is absorbed with treating symptoms, while the latter is focused on preventative healthcare and the treatment of the root cause of the illness.

I, for instance, have been nursing a 'frozen' shoulder for over a year now and have taken anti-inflammatory pills and had cortisone shots with no effect on the problem. On the problem... there is one of my concerns, no effect on the problem, but what about the rest of my body? How has the rest of my body reacted to the chemicals I've swallowed and had injected? Only after the fact, did I learn that the cortisone shots could increase my chances of contracting arthritis in that shoulder in later life. To compound the situation, I remember the specialist warning me that it might not make a difference but 'hell it was worth a try'. It is amazing how much we are willing to do to ourselves on the off chance it might work, just because we have been programmed to believe that doctors always know best.

When I think of people undergoing chemotherapy or radiation treatment, I now imagine a race between the person and the disease to see which one the so-called cure destroys first. Surely some of the methods that come from ancient cultures and from the natural world are worth trying when conventional practices are so horrific?

When I discovered the amazing fact regarding the doctors' strike in Israel, featured earlier, I thought it might be an isolated incidence, but it took little of Steve's research time to uncover other similar stories. In Bogota, Columbia, an eight-week strike resulted in a 35% drop in the death rate. In Los Angeles, during a work slowdown, an 18% drop in death rate was experienced which returned to normal as soon as the medical industry was back working at full strength. [4]

As I head toward my later years (I hate it when people say the 'autumn of life', it makes me feel as if I am losing my leaves), my body seems to be falling apart. A whole host of things keep causing problems: my knees are complaining when I hike my favorite West Coast trails, my prostate is unhappy, my liver dicey, acne rosacea hit a few years ago, and the list goes on. It's at times like this that you start to look at the long haul. Perhaps it's time to look after oneself a little better. So, several years ago I started

---

[4] Reclaiming Our Health; John Robbins

having annual check-ups; you know, heart, lungs, blood pressure, latex and Vaseline-covered finger - the unhappy works - and it turns out I'm passable for my age. I am also lucky that my doctor has an open mind when it comes to treating health problems. He believes in preventative medicine and treats the whole body, not just the symptoms. He has a great philosophy, which goes something like 'if it works keep on doing it'. He has supported me trying various homeopathic preparations (in one particular case with spectacular results), so much so that he now recommends these to all his patients with similar health concerns.

After working with Karen and Ryan for several weeks and going off on several tangents, I managed to finish their business plan. I was now champing at the bit to know more about complementary health practices and specifically about the extraordinary Quantum Xrroid Conscious Interface device. Even more interesting was the possibility of meeting Professor Nelson, although this looked highly unlikely given that he lived in Hungary almost 9,000 km away.

As so often happens karma, or it could have been serendipity, took a hand. I was back in my favorite coffee shop discussing some editorial pieces that Karen and Ryan wanted me to write when Ryan said, "Wouldn't it be great if someone wrote a book on Bill?"

It took me a few seconds before I realized he was referring to Professor Nelson and then when I did, I didn't for one-minute think he was thinking of me as the author. But then he said, "You could write it Simon, we need someone we can trust."

I was, at that time, predominantly a business writer and therefore suggested that rather than me as the author we should ask a ghostwriter friend of mine if he would be interested in writing the book. As it turned out my friend was busy with other work, and he asked why I wasn't going to write it myself? When I couldn't give a satisfactory answer it dawned on me that three people in the last 24 hours had thought I could do it. I seemed outnumbered. Once I got used to the idea, writing a biography of this charismatic figure seemed just what I needed to take me into a whole new sphere of writing. I was only half right; it was to take me into a whole new way of thinking altogether.

TAKING CONTROL

My name is Jodie; I am a patient trying not to become a statistic.
This is my story.

My battle with cancer, the big 'C', has lasted for 6 years so far. I have concentrated my efforts on self-healing, both for mind and body, in the belief that attitude is everything. I have avoided traditional medical intervention, searching instead for alternatives: a flotsam and jetsam mishmash of possibilities either discovered or presented to me like lottery tickets from friends.

Life throws things at us for one reason or another and I chose to accept this disease as a gift: something which would help me work through past emotions and old attitudes. I gave up my power to no one; this was a journey which I would control myself. Deadlines have been given and have passed. 'Two to three weeks' has become several months.

A biofeedback system called the QXCI has made a difference: physically of course, but more importantly, the wealth of subjective information it has given me has been the crowning glory of all my years of intense labor in trying to understand the relationship between my mind and the cancer that invades my body.

The QXCI was recommended by neighbors; their experiences piqued my interest. I was not, however, prepared for what it would do for me. Ted, an experienced QXCI practitioner, explained briefly that the device would read the electromagnetic field in my body by basically hooking up with my subconscious. This device scans the body for thousands of substances, identifies allergies and traumas, whether mental, physical, emotional or spiritual. It then tells you when the traumas happened and where in the body. This QXCI machine measures life-force, willpower, oxygenation, hydration and more. It sends out frequencies to help correct the deficiencies and recommends homeopathic treatments.

Do I believe it?

In my case it located the 'neuronet' in the brain associated with my cancer; I actually saw it on the screen. There was a line, the neuron, connecting it to an organ in my body. The QXCI then sent out frequencies to heal that connection.

I believe that all disease has its roots in attitudinal or emotional trauma and for the last few years I have focused on the core attitudes for this disease. I have dragged up anything and everything I could find that seemed obvious or was hidden. I worked on issues such as anger, resentment, and victimization and some-times felt I was getting close to discovery, but I was never able to make that final breakthrough.

Then the QXCI came into my life. Here was a device linked to a computer that I could ask, "What are my secrets?" It delved into my emotional psyche and discovered three key emotions I battle with. The first I had already recognized, and was trying to deal with, the second I had not recognized but saw clearly when it was pointed out. The third was a bio-emotional conflict which effects my digestion - a weak link since birth. The QXCI sent electrical frequencies through my body to help me heal and my practitioner recommended some homeopathic preparations. These treatments have made an amazing difference.

Why have I taken the path I have - a path that leads away from allopathic medicine? Because I did not want to give up control, control over the direction I wanted to take, control over myself. Putting myself into the hands of traditional medicine was going to mean sacrificing my power to choose. With Ted and the QXCI device, I was in control. When I didn't want to move into a deeper area the computer would get that message and wouldn't take me there. I value the non-invasive method which keeps my free will intact.

Why I am sharing all this? Because it is time for people to take ownership of their lives and demand more. To stop accepting the rhetoric of medical professionals and the pharmaceutical companies that run our medical systems today.

The 'cut, paste, drug and radiate' mentality is one of control and power. It has undermined our health and the environment we live in at every level throughout the world. New sciences, particularly quantum physics, have opened gateways which allow complementary medical disciplines and technologies to come together to identify problems within our bodies and heal us both physically and mentally. Listen to the story of one who has experienced it; it is not futuristic; it is here and now and it is gentle and self-empowering.

BUDAPEST

*I*n 1970 three Americans were on their way to fulfill their destiny by landing on the moon. The rupture of a service-module oxygen tank forced them to circle the moon without landing. Their destiny was now in the hands of others. The aborted landing significantly altered how they would navigate their way back to earth. To get Apollo 13 back on a free-return-to-earth course the navigation system needed to be re-computed in a hurry. It was an almost impossible task which, unbeknownst to many people, fell on the shoulders of a young mathematical genius working for the manufacturer of the 'gyro' system: William Nelson, an unsung hero who played his part in bringing the astronauts home.

Nothing more was said over the next few weeks about Professor Nelson, and I was beginning to think that writing his biography was just another pipe dream. After all, why would he want an unknown author writing his story?

Then out of the blue Karen called to tell me that Bill had agreed to their suggestion and wanted to see me in Budapest. At this stage my high-energy outward self came into conflict with my low-energy, prone to depression, inner self and I started doubting everything: myself for even thinking that I could manage to write this book, Karen and Ryan for some ulterior motive (although I was at a loss to figure out what it could possibly be) and Bill for flying an unknown wannabe author half way round the world just to meet him.

So many times over the next few weeks I almost changed my mind as I found dozens of reasons why I shouldn't go. In the end the one thing that made me take on the challenge was that I could never have lived with myself knowing that I had had the opportunity and not taken it.

Two weeks later I was sat in a Boeing 747 heading across the Atlantic for a meeting that was to change my life.

To say I was nervous is an understatement. I was flying halfway across the world to meet a man who had invented a device that could change the face of medicine, as we know it. This was someone who had taken the early work carried out on energetic medicine in the 1930s and advanced it so much that it was barely recognizable. A man with no less than five doctorates and a Masters degree in counselling psychology, who at the age of eighteen worked on the navigational gyro system for the Apollo 13 Space

Mission, and who, in his twenties, was assistant professor of mathematics at Youngstown State University.

For the third time since take off, I reviewed the information I had got Steve to find for me off the Internet. Professor Nelson's early school days were as impressive as his post-secondary education. My eyes scanned the sheets and I discovered that the man I was travelling to see had demonstrated incredible mathematical and scientific skills as a young child. He maximized the Stanford Binet intelligence test and others at age eight, resulting in a newspaper report that his intelligence was beyond conventional measurement. As I read on I found that he got a perfect score of 800 on his math, physics, chemistry and biology SAT's and attained a 34 on the ACT college test out of a possible 36. He was admitted to Menoa at the age of 16 and in 1972, after God tells him he should rewrite molecular biology, he starts to write the Promorpheus Treatise, which would take a decade to complete. According to the notes, it is still (twenty years later) the most technical and mathematical treatise on life processes and a work that has earned Professor Nelson a Nobel Prize nomination every year since its publication. Who is this man, I ask myself? As the lights go down in the cabin, I put the papers away telling myself I'll finish reading them before I meet the professor.

The flight was uneventful and long and I found myself with a 4-hour layover in Heathrow airport. By this time I was feeling somewhat jaded as my inner time clock fought to adjust to

London time. The airport lounges were busy and there were few places to sit but at last I found what I was looking for, a seat next to an electrical outlet where I could plug in my laptop and settle down for a few hours work. I sat, oblivious to the hustle and bustle around me, planning and reviewing the questions I was going to ask the professor.

When I eventually arrived at the Budapest airport I was tired and somewhat nervous. I was almost prepared for there to be no one to meet me; after all, geniuses are supposed to be forgetful and this was all like a dream anyway. As I walked through customs and into the light grey and black marble of the newly refurbished and highly impressive Ferihegy airport, I scanned the dozens of signs peppered with names held by people lined up at the Customs' exit. Professor Nelson's wife, Ildico, had said that their driver would be there to pick me up and that he would be holding a sign bearing my name. No such name was on any of the proffered signs and although, as a seasoned traveller I was not too perturbed by having to find a hotel for the night, my heart sank a little. This did not bode well and added to my misgivings about travelling all this way to meet with a somewhat eccentric American quantum physicist-biologist who was living in exile in Budapest.

As I put my bags down behind the line of people waiting for passengers from my flight, a longhaired young man hurried passed me with a white card sign and pushed his way forcefully to the front of the melée of people. Something told me this might be the professor's driver so I pushed through the crowd after him and signed for him to turn the card around so that I could see the name. Dr. Nelson's name was scrawled across the card not mine, but it achieved the same result.

Kareem, smiling broadly, introduced himself to me in broken English and hurried me toward - believe it or not - a Ford Aerostar with Ontario license plates. This was just one more indication of how strange everything was in my life now that it included quantum physicists and other such mysteries. Within seconds of pulling away my driver looked slightly panicked and I spotted a police roadblock on the road leading out of the airport. Kareem was frantically putting on his seat belt and shaking his head. I asked what the problem was and he said, "it okay, but Hungarian police not like Romanians." Luckily the police were busy with another driver and we careered past without a care, although if the truth be known my heart was beating harder than it should have been at my time of life. If I had any doubts that my journey was an odyssey of discovery, an intellectual and spiritual quest, a mystery, I think that at that moment they were completely dispelled.

It was around 10:30 p.m. as we left the airport and drove toward town, my driver apologizing constantly for his poor English, which was, however, substantially better than my non-existent Romanian. Conversation centered on the normal pleasantries about family, the journey, some basic facts about Budapest and how long I was staying. I asked how long he had worked for Professor Nelson and over the next few minutes it became clear that the professor's charisma was a definite reality. Kareem was obviously very happy working for Professor Nelson and seemed somewhat in awe of him.

With the lights of downtown beckoning in the distance, we turned off the highway and started to enter a run-down part of the outskirts of the city. Once again the strangeness of the situation struck me. Here I was in a van, at the mercy of a stranger who looked somewhat like a heavy in a Sylvester Stallone movie, being driven through what looked like an unsavory part of an Eastern European town late at night. As Kareem stared down dark alleys looking for god only knows what, I began to feel increasingly uncomfortable as images from 'R' rated movies flashed across my memory. With a sharp turn of the wheel the car bounced up a curb and came to rest outside a couple of boarded-up stores above which a large and dark, post-war tenement building loomed.

The building was gloomy and foreboding, and it was hard to imagine that the highly successful professor lived there. We all have pre-conceived images of people and places and are usually surprised when reality fails to meet expectations. I had somehow imagined the professor living in a fashionable district of Budapest in a dramatic and flamboyant apartment.

Kareem led me up a flight of stairs that I distinctly remember seeing in a 1950s 'B' movie, and said he would go and find the professor. As I followed him, we entered a door that led off a first-floor balcony overlooking a small courtyard, and I found myself in a very ordinary looking hallway, with a kitchen facing me and corridors leading to the right and left. Kareem beckoned me to follow him into the kitchen and began knocking on a door. A few seconds later a head appeared with very wet, long blond hair; this was my first sight of the professor. Not a good start, I thought, disturbing his bath. He suggested that Kareem show me to my room to unpack and he would see me in a few minutes.

It was a comfortable room one floor above the professor's with a television, sofa and bed. The wardrobes were full of women's dresses and I wondered where the owner was. Kareem had pointed to a dining room when we were downstairs and told me that this is where I would be meeting Bill. In a short while I trekked back downstairs and waited nervously in the dining room for what felt like an audience with the Pope.

My second sight of the professor was even more interesting than the first. He swept into the room still damp from the bath, wrapped in a flowing kimono style gown and shook my hand with a firm grip. The next forty minutes or so went past in a blur, as we talked of everything: my trip, my background and energetic medicine; we told jokes and generally got to know each other. By the end of that first session I knew beyond any shadow of a doubt I was dealing with an extraordinary man with a phenomenal mind. Professor Nelson had become Bill, and I looked forward to the many hours we had set aside for me to interview him. We discussed briefly the difference between allopathic and holistic medicine and then about synthetic drugs and the dangers he saw in them. He promised that we would discuss this more the following day. During this early encounter, Bill told me of his dream to have a popular book published on holistic medicine and the QXCI device, a book that explained what it was and why it was important.

So, as I sat with Bill, this most fascinating man, I became hooked. I had to know more about this new medicine and this amazing device that seemed to hold so much promise. If what he was saying was true, then the story had to be told and I wanted to be the one to tell it. It confirmed all my own suspicions and opened up a Pandora's box that I knew I would never be able to shut again. It took my breath away to think of what was happening in the field of traditional medicine: we, the people, had been sold a bill of goods. There were viable alternatives to traditional medical treatments that were not being made readily available to us; even worse, the potential for curing people of serious diseases was being dismissed because the methods didn't fit standard formulas and the narrow-minded thinking of the medical establishment.

That night, as I lay trying to switch off and sleep, I decided that I had to write a book on what the QXCI stood for and to promote the fact that all complementary health techniques should be given the right to a fair hearing for the sake of everyone's good health. This book would provide me with the answers I needed. It would allow me to satisfy my burning desire to promote a better way to provide healthcare. And I had an expert here who was more than willing to share his knowledge and experience with me. What an opportunity!

The apartment block was a hive of activity throughout the night with people coming and going, the hum of voices, doors slamming. I first awoke at 1:40 a.m. and lay listening to the sounds, wondering what was happening. Why was there so much going on? Who were these people? What sort of place was this? My imagination ran riot as it dreamt up a scenario in which the apartment block was some sort of brothel and the nocturnal comings and goings were those of dirty old men and illicit meetings - rooms rented by the hour.

Every time I dozed off it seemed someone else arrived. In truth, I am an incredibly light sleeper and almost anything will wake me. In the cold light of day, the truth was a lot less colorful than the reality portrayed by my overworked imagination. The apartments are occupied by Bill's staff, many of whom are young and enjoy Budapest's night life to its fullest. In addition the balcony outside my door was a favorite place to stand and smoke and talk.

Anyway, even if the truth is a lot less exciting, I am going to have difficulty sleeping here. I might have to consider moving into a hotel. All that can wait - later today I start interviewing Bill.

When I met with Bill the next day, he was deep in conversation with Franco, a Spanish doctor, who with two colleagues had come to work with Bill for a week or two. Franco had a long list of queries and suggestions regarding the software program that is at the heart of the QXCI device, and Bill was going through each one, methodically explaining how a particular screen worked or agreeing that a glitch had been discovered which should be corrected in the upgrade he was currently working on. I watched for two hours, as absorbed as they were in their work. It was not until that moment that I realized the incredible complexity and power of the system. Until then I thought the device was like the 'point and probe' biofeedback devices I had read about while researching energetic medicine prior to coming to Budapest. In comparison, the QXCI was like a Pentium 5, while these devices were 286 computers running on DOS! The power and scope of the device was phenomenal; the fact that one man could have developed this amazing piece of medical software was miraculous. At some stage I would have to ask him how he had managed this feat.

Later in the day Bill and I managed to get some time together and I set out my tape recorder on the kitchen table. As I sat there gathering my thoughts, I was struck by the fact that I was interviewing what can only be described as a genius, in his kitchen, while a pretend monster, in the form of Bill's very attractive wife Ildiko, was chasing their young son. As time went on, various staff members wandered in and out, supplying food and drink to us. Two floors above us was the heart of Bill's empire, the Maitreya Institute, where the QXCI was manufactured. The paradox, which only fully struck me sometime later, was that on one side Bill is what I would call a 'WYSIWYG' (what you see is what you get): he doesn't try to impress you with possessions, just his mind. Yet another side of him is flamboyant in the extreme, theatrical and more fitting to a Noel Coward play. His ego is probably as big as his intellect, but this somehow only adds to the charisma of the man. I have yet to meet anyone who is labeled a genius who hasn't got an ego the size of Texas. He is an irrepressible straight talker who is a thorn in the side of anyone whose house is built of anything but good solid brick. People who confront him with an idea or philosophy that isn't founded on sound principles will find that he can huff and puff and blow their house down with an ease that is frightening. People who have experienced this side of Bill dislike the fact that he actually enjoys blowing people's houses of straw down; it is his life's work and he is very, very good at it. Many of us don't suffer fools gladly, but to Bill they are like a red rag to a bull.

As I listened to Bill talk, I was captivated by the strength of his convictions. It was obvious that he truly believes in his crusade to expose and thereby temper the corporate goliaths and make them release their stranglehold on traditional medicine. And to get them to accept the fact that complementary medical practices are not only here to stay, but that an unstoppable groundswell of public opinion is rising like a tsunami to engulf their profit-centered, narrow-minded, outdated thinking.

His hatred of drug companies is well known and he has spoken out against them on numerous occasions, so much so that he fears reprisals. The initial impetus for his private war against the pharmaceutical industry originates from the fact that his son, now in his early twenties, suffered brain damage from one of Thalidomide's successors. Since then however, he has seen the drug barons get richer and richer by synthesizing natural substances into name brand drugs. My research into this field later confirmed many times over what Bill had been telling me. As an example: despite the enormous amount of money spent on drugs, in New York City 10.8 infants out of 1,000 die before their first birthday, while in Shanghai, China, the rate is only 9.9. On top of this, life expectancy in New York is 73 years for whites and 70 for people of colour, while in Shanghai the figure is 75.5. Shanghai is an overpopulated and polluted third world country. It has a per capita income of $350 and spends only $38 per person annually on medical care. New York spends $3,000! [5] It would seem that good health is not necessarily based entirely on who can spend the most money, or indeed make the most.

---

[5] Reclaiming Our Health, John Robbins ISBN:0915811804

Occasionally, we learn something that makes so much sense we smack our forehead and say, 'of course, it makes so much sense, why didn't I think of that before?'

In Bill's kitchen, in a suburb of Budapest, this happened to me. Bill told me the story of a frog. It is a very small frog and it is indigenous to a certain region of Eastern Europe; it secretes a greenish substance that has great healing powers. The great thing about this wonderful material is that it requires little or no processing before being given to a patient. When the drug companies learned about this marvellous, natural pharmaceutical preparation they set about immediately trying to recreate or duplicate it synthetically in their laboratories. When Bill asked them why they would go to all this effort when they could just breed the frogs and harvest their secretions, the reply came back: "But somebody could steal our frogs and breed them themselves!" At this stage of the story I was a little slow on the uptake (I blame it on jet-lag), so Bill explained, "It's like this Simon. If a drug company can synthesize a natural chemical they can get a patent for it; this is impossible to do for a naturally occurring substance. It's all about money."

The ramifications of this started to dawn on me pretty quickly. Drug companies didn't always need to recreate what was natural, but had to do so to protect themselves and to allow them to own the preparation exclusively. With my old business consultant's hat on, this made a whole lot of sense and I could sympathize with the drug companies; after all they had to make a profit right? But then I started to think, how much profit and at whose expense?

Bill continued, "Simon, would you eat synthetic food?"

I shook my head and replied with a grin, "Does McDonald's count?"

He went on to explain that in Ohio, his home state, experiments were carried out into the manufacture of a synthetic fat that would not be absorbed by the body; this would be a great aid in preventing obesity. The problem was that in trials 85 percent of people got bowel cancer or colitis. Who would knowingly eat synthetic foods? But we ingest synthetic drugs like candy on a regular basis, trillions of dollars of them.

This got me thinking again about my concerns over standard medical treatment. A friend had recently been given a drug, which resulted in him having to make a trip to emergency. He ended up hospitalized in a serious condition for several frightening days. Many months later he was still not able to return to work.

One of Steve's pieces of research came to mind. An American study carried out at a university hospital revealed that 36% of 815 consecutive patient admissions had an iatrogenic illness, which is an illness resulting from medical treatment and not as a natural consequence of the patient's disease.[6] One report[7], using conservative estimates from studies carried out in Colorado and Utah and extrapolating them over the 33.6 million admissions to hospitals in the United States in 1997, shows that iatrogenic illness attributes to more deaths than the eighth leading cause of death.

My previous inbred cynicism regarding the credibility of complementary medicine, or as I had until recently known it - 'alternative' medicine, was gradually being transferred to what we know of as traditional medicine. Most complementary medical treatments have been around for thousands of years, so it seems strange to me that the newer, industrialized, technical and synthetic system has adopted the word traditional for something that is anything but that.

As I discovered more from Bill about the political world of medicine, I came to the conclusion that this would make a great television drama series. Not the E.R. or Chicago Hope versions but a gritty, down to earth series about the politics and infighting between two separate belief systems: complementary medicine and traditional. The victim would be the patient. There would be heroes on both sides as they fought for the middle ground where

[6] Steel, Knight; Gertman, Paul M; Crescenzi, Caroline; et al. Iatrogenic Illness on a General medical Service at a University Hospital. New England Journal of Medicine 304:638-642, 1981.
[7] Centers for Disease Control and Prevention (National Center for Health Statistics). Deaths: Final Data for 1997. National Vital Statistics Report 47(19):27, 1999.

the two disciplines would work hand in hand for the greater good of mankind, their efforts constantly being thwarted by politics and those individuals and corporations whose wealth depended on the status quo. It would have industrial espionage, doctors fighting for the right to medical freedom, medical quacks giving both sides a bad name and patients fighting for their rights.

Bill brought me back from thoughts of fame and fortune as the screenplay writer of this television series just as I got up to accept my Emmy.

"Simon, traditional medical practitioners and complementary medical practitioners think very differently. Academically and philosophically they are poles apart." Bill leant back in his chair and I realized how much his students at Youngstown must have enjoyed his lectures.

"On the one side, a doctor has to have mathematics, chemistry and physics to get into medical school. He or she is taught statistics and logical thinking, the need for studies, research, facts and figures and a mathematical process that decides what is good and what is bad. They are taught the need to have studies involving hundreds, if not thousands, of people before they even start to give serious consideration to a new treatment."

I could see that Bill was enjoying himself; he was on a roll, so I just nodded while he continued.

"Complementary practitioners however, are often those people who might have become doctors, but couldn't or didn't want to live in the world of mathematical probability. They approach things differently; they comprehend things by listening, by mood, by case histories, by feeling. They do not want to be restricted by such a rigid system of thinking."

This all made sense to me as I reached across the table and poured myself another cup of green tea.

"If several patients tell them that a certain treatment works and they have corroboratory evidence, they will try it out, as long as it is safe to do so. They don't need several years of testing while hundreds of people die waiting and the cost of the drug increases to the point where more than half the world can no longer afford it."

I remembered that in many cases, where a drug has gone through extensive testing in one country and found to be safe, it is still not allowed to be used in another country until they test it themselves.

Bill stopped talking and looked at me to see if I understood. I nodded and asked, "But doesn't that mean they are in danger of giving someone medicine that could be harmful."

Bill shook his head. "Not at all, holistic medical practitioners are highly trained individuals and would never suggest a treatment that wasn't well known, tried and tested. Remember Simon, most of the preparations recommended are naturally occurring substances and have been used for thousands of years."

"So," I said. "In reality they have probably been tested more thoroughly than many of the so called safe drugs?"

"Exactly," replied Bill with a smile on his face. "Exactly!"

As if by some strange quirk of karma, Bill's son Daniel appeared in the kitchen, someone whose life was changed by a so-called statistically safe and tested drug.

All of a sudden, I felt tired. Being in Bill's company was incredibly stimulating; his knowledge of the medical world from the perspective of both the traditional and complementary side was outstanding, but my mind was reeling from all the information I had absorbed. He was obviously a unique individual and I was looking forward to tomorrow's session when I was to learn more about the history of energetic medicine, and the technology behind the Quantum Xrroid Conscious Interface. Bill had also promised to provide me with some real-life case studies to illustrate the power of the device.

I spent that evening alone in a restaurant in downtown Budapest. I needed some space to reflect, and to put some distance between the powerful man I had spent the day with and myself. I needed perspective and I needed to do some research before tomorrow.

As I lay in bed that night I thought about how important the interrelationship between traditional and complementary medicine was to the world. Without doubt things were going to change over the next few years, as the groundswell of public opinion forced itself into the consciousness of politicians and those to whom healthcare was a source of great wealth. A comment made by Bill earlier in the day rose to the forefront of my mind, "If I were you Simon I would sell my drug company shares."

My fast track education in energetic medicine and biofeedback devices like the QXCI was becoming a roller-coaster ride of epic proportions. I thought back to how it all started when I met my two young friends in a coffee shop thousands of miles away and where it had brought me to, and where it was yet to take me. From skeptic to believer, from someone who had never experienced complementary medicine to an avid proponent of it? I wasn't yet sure. I am not, and never will be, a 'born-again' anything, so with the help of Steve I will be researching and verifying the facts wherever I can. I am beginning to think that I will need to retain another researcher to interview QXCI patients and practitioners. I met a young lady called Hannah a few weeks ago who will fit the bill perfectly.

As complex beings we are searching for many things in our lives, the most obvious being wealth, health and happiness. Happiness most often comes from having the first two leavened with some level of spiritual direction and peace. Given the choice between wealth and health most of us, if we thought about it, would settle for health, but we need help in achieving and maintaining it. We don't expect our governments to make us wealthy, in fact we expect the opposite, as they continue to tax us in every imaginable way. We do, however, expect them to help us remain healthy by providing a basically healthy environment with clean, unpolluted drinking water and access to decent medical care. In essence, we have been promised these things as an integral part of our contract with the people we elect to run our countries for us. I was coming to the realization that traditional medicine has never completely fulfilled its promise to me, or anyone else for that matter.

As I drift off to sleep, I realize that I am in the privileged position of being able to interview a key player in the future of world healthcare. Tomorrow, I will rise early and take a look at Budapest. Karen and Ryan are due to arrive later in the day and add their perspective to this fascinating story. It will be an interesting day.

THE QXCI EXPERIENCED

My name is Hannah. I am Simon's researcher.

My meeting with Penny had surprised me; she was so intense, so believable. Everything she said had resonated with me and now writing up my notes for Simon I feel I have become emotionally attached to the story in a way I would never have believed. I must and will, however, stay focused and unbiased in my research.

I have made an appointment to experience the QXCI for myself. I will not rely solely on what others tell me: I need to put things into perspective and the only way I can think of doing this is to become a patient.

My thoughts drifted back to the interview I had with Simon for this contract. My first impressions were of an interesting character with a strong and sometimes overpowering personality. I was attracted to his energy and enthusiasm that sweeps you up like a surfer's perfect wave, but remember balancing this with a sense of caution about being out of my depth. He seemed to feed on his own adrenaline, pumping it up like the Incredible Hulk until he could hardly contain it.

However, I also saw in Simon, somewhat of a lost soul. Outwardly he was confident, an extrovert bursting with a force that didn't seem quite under control. But I sensed someone who was searching for something, a meaning to life, a purpose, perhaps even a faith. In many ways we were opposites, but then I could see great similarities.

Simon didn't so much interview me as sell me the job, all the while monitoring my level of enthusiasm. He must have seen what he was looking for because by the end of our meeting I was a signed-up, card-carrying member of the project.

I consider my self an intelligent and grounded person and knew I could do the job Simon had outlined. The thought of investigating the world of this incredible device, which seemed far too good to be true, was just the sort of challenge I needed.

I grew up in a small farming community in the Canadian prairies from Viking stock, and became tall and strong with long blonde hair radiating Scandinavian good health. My parents tell me I was an intuitive child with a knowing way that showed itself in a spiritual awareness beyond my years. Unlike other kids who read books like Charlotte's Web and The Incredible Journey, I grew up reading books such as Love, Medicine and Miracles, The Road Less Travelled and almost anything on alternative health. I read about Buddhism and Taoism too. As a teenager I worked in an alternative bookstore which allowed me to read my way through entire libraries of books on just about every metaphysical subject.

Later, to use a euphemism, I went 'off the tracks' and ended up experimenting with just about any and every substance I could get my hands on. Life on the streets, glamorous perhaps at first to a disillusioned and rebellious teen, becomes a life of hunter and hunted depending on the day and the circumstances. Street violence, drug abuse and ill health become a way of life. A victim-and-blame mentality comes with the territory. This was the life I lived for a period, in turns enjoying its excitement, rebellion and tenuous camaraderie, and in turns being sickened by its degradation. Perhaps there was a need in my psyche to reach rock bottom before being able to find my real place in the world and discover the reason for my existence.

A few years ago, in my mid-thirties, I turned myself around and now use the intense experiences of the past to fashion a future which involves understanding the gap between traditional and alternative belief structures and a continuous search for truth. I seek a future where my existence on this planet matters and the effect I have is one of positive influence on the world's karma. Everything we do has an effect on something else, either pleasant or unpleasant, positive or negative, like the ripples caused by the smallest pebble thrown into a pond. It would seem that the

QXCI has the power to effect the lives of many people and do great good in the right hands, and if given the opportunity. There are some though for whom quantum ripples, free spirits out of their direct control, are a threat. I take Simon's trust in me to seek out the truth very seriously.

As I set off to visit Penny's clinic not really knowing what to expect, my mind was full of all that I had heard from Penny and Simon about the QXCI and its somewhat eccentric inventor. I imagined the thousands of people who every day made this journey to one of more than 3,000 other QXCI practitioners: patients fighting illness and others, first-timers perhaps, with hidden cancers lying in wait, ready to ambush their lives. People suffering with unknown maladies hoping beyond hope that this electronic device will interpret their body's signals more effectively than the skill, knowledge and experience of a fallible human.

Many of us treat doctors like gods, but they are human with all the human failings that hang off that status like branches on a tree: bias, ego, prejudice, politics, greed, avarice and bigotry. I have always thought of doctors as fat-cats, overpaid technicians who rarely keep their skills up to date. They are like computers running an operating system several years, in many cases decades, out of date. In my region recently, doctors withdrew their services to the public during a fight with government about how increased funding budgets were to be spent and how future disputes were to be resolved. The health and well-being of their patients were put on hold while they fought to protect their lifestyle. Of course, not all doctors are like this, many are far more enlightened and look at medicine from a more holistic perspective - be it medically, practically or politically. These represent the future I dream of: where traditional medicine embraces alternative breakthroughs such as the QXCI, and work together to test and improve them for the greater good of mankind, not to worship the God of Mammon.

I can see why there is a move toward alternative therapies, even those primarily controlled by an electronic device and its computer partner. So, as I drew up at Penny's clinic, I recognized my own preconceptions, which favored the type of experience I was about to have, and realized that I would have to attempt a more balanced approach. Her clinic was in the basement of her small unpretentious house in a mature neighborhood full of flowers and trees and birdsong. Cottage gardens abounded, which reminded me of old picture books of English villages published in the fifties. I almost expected Mrs. Marples to peek out from over a privet hedge and wish me a 'good morning' tinged with a healthy mix of civility and nosiness.

Inside, the waiting room was quiet and calm with soft music playing. A table, a few chairs and alternative health magazines were spread on the coffee table. Its ordinariness struck me as I realized I had expected something different, but for the life of me couldn't think what. Penny came out of what I suspected was the consulting room and said she would be with me in a few minutes. As I sat waiting I wondered whether I should try to test the machine, and by inference Penny.

A few minutes later a man in his early thirties came out of the consulting room and said, "You next for being zapped?" I nodded, unsure whether I liked the idea of being zapped: it sounded like something that happened to flies when they were drawn into that device with the strange blue light you often see in restaurants. I wonder sometimes if the ones that survive tell their friends, "I saw this light at the end of a tunnel, it was beautiful and I was being drawn towards it..."

Penny welcomed me into her inner sanctum which she shared with the QXCI. I could hardly wait to see it for myself.

"Good to see you again Hannah. I so enjoyed our lunch a few weeks ago. Have you had chance to speak to any other practitioners or patients yet?"

As I scanned the room I explained that I wanted to wait until I had experienced the QXCI myself so that I could better understand what I was talking about. She smiled and asked me to take a seat in a very inviting black leather recliner. As I lay back she attended to her computer, closing windows, opening others and generally taking on the appearance of a NASA scientist preparing for the launch of a space shuttle. Dozens of complicated screens appeared and disappeared until finally a questionnaire was left on the monitor.

Ah! I thought, this is where I tell her everything about my health and the machine magically agrees with me. In fact, the questions were fairly general and although they gave Penny a guide as to the areas which might be issues for me, they still left a lot of room for interpretation. The QXCI device itself was a small grey box with cables going in and out of it; it could not have been more ordinary. At first I felt a little disappointed and then it occurred to me that the truly great things in life don't have to be flashy and in your face.

Penny strapped a headband onto me followed by wrist and ankle bands and asked me to just relax. I could see the computer screen flashing through several screens and caught sight of a butterfly among many other colorful images. After a minute or so I relaxed and seemed to sink deeply into the chair vaguely wondering where she got it from and whether I could afford one.

After a short while she announced that the QXCI had carried out its 'handshake' with me, and the preliminary report was to hand. I was immediately astounded by the device's accuracy. Every one of my health concerns including those that had not come up during the questionnaire were identified. What totally blew me away was the fact that it told me that during gestation week 17, I suffered a trauma. Here was a machine that was somehow so sensitive that it could pick up some sort of variation in energy patterns in the weeks before I was even born. I know for a fact that my mother very nearly miscarried me in week 17 of her pregnancy.

If that was not enough, I had long suspected that my body contained abnormally high levels of metals and the machine indicated high levels of mercury in my system. It was gratifying to have one's own intuition proved correct.

Penny could see that that I was impressed, and asked me what I thought so far.

I told her that it matched a lot of my beliefs already and that I was in tune with the fact that everything is energy in the Universe. We discussed my past experiences in alternative health and the fact that I had a fair degree of knowledge of the body and things such as chakras. I very much believe that we have a spiritual body as well as a physical body and that our spiritual bodies are composed of vibrations of light which are structured in such a way as to create different centers. This gives us two existences - one spiritual and one physical.

What excited me most about my experience with the device was its emotional readings and the way it looked at my aura. As the computer screen reflected the signals from the device it seemed to be talking to me in a language I understood; it related to me here and now. Penny identified that my root chakra was way off centre and this was consistent with my recent difficulties with pre-menstrual tension and my reproductive system in general.

Without some knowledge and acceptance of alternative health practices I might have found the experience confusing and I could see that some people might think it all so much mumbo-jumbo. It would be good for practitioners to spend some time explaining the QXCI experience to people who have only ever experienced, or believed in, traditional medicine in the past. Cell phones for instance are truly a phenomenon to many people. They take our words, turn them into energy, which then travels invisibly and instantly over long distances to be reassembled in a tiny device thousands, even tens of thousands of miles away. On a less technological note, alternative medical therapies such as acupuncture, acupressure and chiropracty have become an accepted part of the arsenal of medical treatments offered by traditional doctors. The leap of faith required to embrace the QXCI has, over the years, become a small jump and in the future it will be a mere step.

Penny suggested that I relax and let the QXCI work on my chakras. She dimmed the lights, and music specially developed for the healing programs that are part of the software package started to envelop me.

As the device worked its magic on me and I drifted into a somnambulant state, I wondered whether this truly incredible device was way before its time. Then I realized that of course it was. Like so many other things that need faith, those that are open to it will find it and those that have a closed mind will never be convinced. So be it.

Back in the car I reviewed the experience from a slightly different perspective, one that was less influenced by the moment. The experience for me was very positive, but how much of that was due to my openness to this type of diagnosis and treatment? I wondered how Simon would get on with the machine? How different would his experience be and how much do the results depend on belief? I remember Simon telling me that Bill had said that the patient has to take responsibility for his or her own body; the QXCI cannot help them if they won't themselves. For people new to anything other than pills and potions, the quick fixes in the traditional medical practitioners arsenal, the QXCI can be a lot to take in at first. It challenges and strains the more traditional belief systems.

The device can do it all, it's that clever, but it really is at its best when the practitioner has a sound knowledge of the way it works, along of course, with superior counselling skills. The complexity and power of the device would concern me if inexperienced practitioners were to use it; its power should not be underestimated.

Although the QXCI is clever, a practitioner could, in theory, have little or no experience of human anatomy and physiology. The device can assess the patient's body, prescribe homeopathic preparations and deliver energetic treatment. For a moment, I sit back and imagine the faces of doctors being told that a machine could now do their job and they were no longer needed, except perhaps in a support role. It would be like movie theatre projectionists who recently have discovered that their job no longer needs most of the technical skills they learned when they took up their trade. Over the last few years they have seen their previously high wages drop significantly as they have become little more than button pushers.

The traffic on the way home was heavy and I found myself studying my fellow commuters. I started to think about the many illnesses they suffered from, knowingly or unknowingly. Our bodies are highly complex pieces of machinery which do not come with a manual. Many of us know more about our car than we do about our body. The QXCI has the power to change that by empowering us with knowledge and an extensive line by line assessment of every aspect of our physical, spiritual and emotional well-being.

At last we have access to a manual of our unique system, a guide to optimum performance. It can tell us if we are feeding it the correct fuel and what we should avoid, what areas are in need of attention and which are performing just fine. I could imagine the QXCI immediately focusing on Simon's over-worked adrenal system!

I saw, up ahead, an old beat up car pumping out black smoke and as I got closer I could see the rust eating away at the doors and wheel arches. The car looked unloved, its owner abusing it day in and day out, but still expecting it to work. By the look and smell of the sooty smoke its days were numbered. Some of us treat our bodies like that, abusing them until they break down, ignoring all the warning signs along the way.

It concerned me that people might think that the QXCI was a cure-all and that using it absolved them of having to take ownership and responsibility for their body. Nothing could be further from the truth! Bill Nelson's teachings clearly promote that people need to work with the device and improve their diet, take exercise, make lifestyle changes and look to homeopathic remedies to assist them rather than the chemical potions peddled by the pharmaceutical companies. The QXCI partners with people in a contract of health, where they are every bit as responsible as it is for the miracles it performs.

That night I slept better than I had for as long as I can remember. My body seemed balanced and I was in harmony with the universe. As I slept, I dreamed I was a butterfly drying my wings in readiness for my first flight, anticipating that first taste of nectar and the freedom and responsibility of life lived as an integral part of the universe. Then, as my wings pushed down and then up again, I saw a chain reaction caused by the displacement of air. This was built upon by other forces which combined with thousands of like minds and came to rest against the yellow, green and red fabric of a child's kite hundreds of miles away. I saw the child's face, creased with delight and joy, looking toward the heavens and somehow knew the child's name was Destiny. This moment would live on in her memory and because of it she would do great good in the world. All because of a butterfly's first flight.

THE NELSON PRINCIPLES OF HEALING

Budapest

Sleep eluded me for most of the night as I tossed and turned, the events of the last few days fighting their way to the forefront of my mind. At 4:30 a.m. I started to write in my journal.

I am awake again. Voices drifting up from the courtyard below disturbed me an hour or so ago. What on earth are people doing at such a miserable hour? I look out of the window but cannot see them so many floors below, their voices rebounding and reverberating off the concrete-and-glass echo chamber of rooms which surround my own. Hotel rooms are soulless places, cocoons for people in limbo caught willingly or unwillingly between destinations, distinctive only by a brevity of mediocre art.

Now I sit here listening to the grinding and creaking and bonging of hotel pipes, like ghosts travelling, hidden in walls and floors. I am beginning to regret leaving Bill's apartment block, it's not a lot quieter here and the problem is mine, not the noise. I have to get some treatment for my light sleeping - perhaps the QXCI can help. Perhaps I need to review the speed at which I live life - invest in myself, my health, my sanity.

Breakfast in the hotel was a grand affair, I was so glad I had decided to eat in the hotel rather than find a café? somewhere. The buffet was extensive and I decided to break my normal habit when staying in a hotel and turn my back on the traditional English cooked breakfast, or at least Hungary's particular version of it. Instead, I helped myself to three different kinds of bread and a selection of salamis, cheeses, olives, peppers and other delicacies. Well, when in Rome, and all that. The hotel dining room contained an interesting mix of Europeans and I could hear as many languages as there were types of bread, an eclectic mix of nationalities and class. Lovers with fingers touching across the table, families with rambunctious children excited by unfamiliar surroundings and unlimited sugar, business people dressed formerly with briefcases and the suave, superior look that comes with familiarity. I smiled at the man at the next table and we struck up a brief conversation, long enough for me to discover he had driven from Italy on business for a few days. I reflected on how many countries were within easy driving distance from Hungary, on how many cultures lived cheek by jowl interacting with each other on a constantly changing basis, and the value of that interface. Then I thought back to home on Vancouver Island and smiled at the memory of a story told to me by a friend shortly after I arrived from England. It highlighted the sheer size of Canada. He had received a call from a cousin in London, England alerting him to the fact that their son was arriving in Toronto the following week. Would he meet him at the airport please? After a brief pause, my friend said, "Why don't you pick him up, you're closer."

After breakfast I walked west from my hotel along a wide street, a slightly shabby tree-lined boulevard. Adjacent to my hotel a grandiose and imposing building took up a city block, it appeared to be a museum of some kind, a stark contrast to the neon-lit strip-club directly opposite the front doors of the hotel, which offered hotel guests free entry but at what cost?

Budapest would continue to be a city of opposites for me, drab buildings backlit by white castles and palaces, a tired, poor looking people with cell phones permanently attached to the side of their heads. It is such an interesting dichotomy that a western luxury item has provided affordable communications opportunities to countries lacking a sophisticated and cost effective telecommunications infrastructure. It occurred to me that the QXCI was itself providing a cost-effective healthcare alternative.

Further on I came to a major intersection and turned left, just wandering, getting a feel for the place. As it was Sunday and very cold, the streets were quiet with relatively few people braving the elements. I could see a massive bridge ahead, which according to my guidebook was called the Chain Bridge and was built to the plans of William Tierney Clark, a British engineer. A Scot called Adam Clark built the bridge over a period of ten years, from 1839 to 1849. I decided to walk toward it.

The River Danube splits the city in two, on one side lies Buda and on the other Pest; I wondered which side I was on and then remembered that the castle district was in Buda, which meant I was in Pest. The view from the centre of the bridge was spectacular and looked across Budapest with its magnificent architectural heritage. The castle district sits on Castle Hill, some sixty metres above the Danube, and is Budapest's pride and joy. Standing here in the middle of the bridge I feel very lonely, not just because I am in a strange country, but because something or someone is missing from my life.

Early in the afternoon I walked to Bill's house, as arranged, to resume our conversations and to meet up with Karen and Ryan. When I arrived Bill was in the kitchen drinking green tea and I took a place beside him. One of his staff immediately placed a cup and saucer, lemon slices and a napkin beside me. I poured myself a cup of tea and looked at Professor Nelson. He has apparently traced his ancestry back to Admiral Horatio Nelson; the familiarity and power of personality had not escaped me.

He broke into my thoughts, and no doubt my visual study of him, to say, "I'd like you to write a book about the QXCI first rather than about me. Not that I don't want you to write the biography later. I have a story which needs to be told, both an inspirational story and an expos? of all that is wrong with the world of traditional medicine and the people that get rich from it. But all that can wait. What I want first is a book that lets people know there is another way and that the QX offers an alternative to the standard diagnostic and therapeutic systems using energetic medicine or bio-resonance therapy currently on the market."

I was glad to hear that Bill had picked up on his earlier suggestion of doing a book on the QXCI device. It would be a fascinating project which would give me an opportunity to study the great man's work before studying the man himself. I had been nodding enthusiastically as he had been speaking and now asked, "But what is the real difference between the QXCI and all the other devices on the market?"

"Well, in basic terms the QX diagnoses and treats in one simultaneous operation allowing for auto focusing of therapy and diagnosis." He looked at me to see if I understood. Although I tried to look intelligent, I was soon to learn that Bill, the teacher, could tell in an instant when someone hadn't really understood.

"Okay Simon, look at it this way. Other devices on the market rely on the practitioner to set the treatment modalities. But this is like picking up a manual camera and expecting it to automatically be in focus for what we want to photograph. It is highly unlikely that this will be the case. The QX, when hooked up to a computer, auto-focuses the therapy by adjusting the system modalities to the patient. The system uses a fuzzy number system to adjust the therapy in the same way that an auto-focus camera works out the distance it is away from the object. All this is outlined in my work 'Promorpheus', which details the mathematics of shape transfer."

I nodded in what I hoped was a knowing way, a nod that was intended to portray that I not only understood, but that the 'Promorpheus Treatise' would be the number one item on my Christmas list. In reality, I was starting to piece together enough elements of information to genuinely say that I understood, in a very basic way, where the QXCI was in the pecking order of biofeedback devices.

"What I probably need to do before I explain what the QX really is and what it does, is to outline the Nelson Principles of Healing. Once you understand what I believe in, your understanding of the device will come a lot easier. This is a complicated device which has taken me most of my life to develop; it is not surprising that people don't understand it immediately or that some even distrust it. When I try to explain it to most people their eyes glaze over - I don't know why. I really believe that I am simplifying it tremendously, but still seem to have trouble bringing my explanation down to a level that people who haven't studied quantum physics or quantum molecular biology can grasp. What I need Simon, is for you to take my words and put them down in such a way that people will be able to understand what I am trying to achieve, and to become familiar enough with the device to want to try it, either as a practitioner or patient."

I am sure he saw my eyes widen as the sheer magnitude of the task sunk in.

We sat there for a few moments in a surreal silence that was suddenly broken by Bill's son being chased through the house once again by Ildiko, this time bearing down on him with a toy dinosaur. Here we were talking of quantum biology surrounded by family life in a Budapest kitchen so ordinary as to be extraordinary.

We decided to have a break and I asked if I could use a computer to check my e-mail. Up in the offices of the Maitreya Institute things seemed a little more balanced and I felt more in control. After checking my messages and replying to those that were urgent, I did a little research on this new technology using some of the new buzz words I had noted down over the last couple of days: fascinating words like biofeedback, vibrational medicine, electroacupuncture. Within a few minutes I came across an article by Hans Larsen, editor and publisher of International Health

News. According to his biography he has a Masters degree in chemical engineering and studied with Nobel prize-winner Professor Henrik Dam, who discovered Vitamin K. His interest in alternative medicine and biochemistry was evident from his fascinating web site. I decided to look and see whether he had written anything on biofeedback devices. He described the work of Professor William Tiller of Stanford University, who believes that chemical reactions and balances in the body are controlled by internal and external electromagnetic fields. These fields are in turn affected by mental or subtle energy fields. As I thought about this for a few seconds, I realized that this would mean that our thoughts could affect our body chemistry. As I read on, Mr. Larsen explained that biofeedback is an accepted medical therapy which demonstrates that our thoughts are exceptionally powerful, that we can learn how to control bodily functions that are normally dealt with by our subconscious. The article went on to describe how biofeedback measures and displays skin conductivity, finger temperature, muscle tension and brain waves.

I opened a new window on the Internet browser and, using my favorite search engine Google, scanned a few more articles on biofeedback and came up with the name Dr. Rheinhold Voll. Apparently in the early 1950s he discovered that the electrical conductivity of our skin increases significantly at acupoints throughout our body. He also found out that each acupoint has an exact conductivity value when we are healthy. Identifying whether higher or lower levels of conductivity exist enables a biofeedback device to assess our health. Since Dr. Voll's time many more electroacupuncture devices have been developed and have proved to be highly effective, not only in diagnosing the health of patients but also in treatment. I discovered that Russian cosmonauts in space are monitored using these devices. Going back to Hans Larsen's excellent site I was surprised to discover that he mentioned the QXCI in glowing terms, referring to it as a truly astonishing piece of equipment!

One of Professor Nelson's staff leaned over my shoulder at this point and said in excellent English, although with a thick accent, "I see you are reading about vibrational medicine and electroacupuncture." I looked up and nodded, and he put a hand on my shoulder, "This is what Bill believes, that we should adapt the way we think, the way we treat our bodies, and modify the subtle energies in our bodies so that we heal ourselves before disease takes over and we are faced with traditional medicine's cut and drug philosophy."

I wrote down the URL for the sites I had visited and planned to learn more about what Dr. Larsen had to say on the subject later.

Bill had been busy in my absence working on the new update for the QXCI and was just finishing off a conversation with the group of visiting Spaniards as I walked in. "Ah Simon!" he exclaimed as he saw me hovering, "Where were we?"

"We were discussing the Nelson Principles of Healing."

His eyes lit up as if he had just cast his gaze on a loved one.

"Yes, you should understand the basic belief system behind all of this, otherwise you will be lost."

I sat silent, waiting for the great man to continue. I looked behind him through the window and out onto a park, a bleak square of dirt surrounded by barren trees. In summer it might be a delightful children's playground, but today it was a cold and tired looking place surrounded by grey buildings. The disparity between the monochromatic outer world and the colorful, multi-dimensional world this character epitomized was not lost on me. I felt like one of the children in the novel The Lion, the Witch and the Wardrobe where, during a game of hide and seek, they go into a wardrobe, push aside an old overcoat and enter a strange and exciting new world. Here they experience wondrous things and experience new paradigms.

"I believe," Bill said, waking me out of my day-dream, "that we first need to remove or reduce the cause of disease. We need to make the patient take responsibility for his or her own present, past and future behavior. Responsibility for separating himself or herself from the cause of the disease is the responsibility of the diseased person. True medicine should be holistic; it is a cooperative relationship between all those involved in a person's wellbeing. Holistic medicine looks at the whole person and analyzes their physical, emotional, nutritional, environmental and spiritual lifestyle values."

I nodded; here was something I knew a little about. I was no stranger to taking a long look at my own health by assessing every aspect of myself. Of course, I have never really done much about it as it meant too much of a lifestyle change, one that I have never been willing to make. Perhaps, I thought, I should listen and learn.

Bill continued, "When we talk of holistic medicine, we do not mean something that excludes what people refer to as traditional medicine but rather something that includes all diagnosis and treatment modalities and even, in some cases, drugs and surgery if there are no adequate alternatives."

This made me sit up, "You mean that although in many cases traditional medical practitioners will not prescribe alternative treatments, holistic practitioners will indeed recommend or suggest more mainstream approaches."

"Of course Simon, that is what holistic means. It focuses on education and responsibility; it offers choice." He let that sink in for a few seconds and then said, "But I don't want to get hung up on definitions at this stage; I want you to understand some more of the basic principles so that tomorrow we can start to talk about the QX device itself." I settled myself in my chair knowing that the next hour or so was going to be a learning experience of immense proportions.

All of a sudden there was a lot of noise from outside and I could hear Kareem telling someone to follow him. The door opened and Kareem entered, followed by Karen and Ryan. The next few minutes were taken up with hugs and kisses, as we were all re-united.

Bill's staff materialized again and plates of food and pots of green tea arrived. The volume in the kitchen rose as everyone tried to talk at once and several conversations took place simultaneously. Ildiko disappeared and reappeared a few seconds later with gifts for Karen's little girl, Destiny, and for Bill's and Ildiko's youngest son. The decibel level took on new proportions as the two children squealed in delight and started to chase each other through the apartment. Once again it struck me as incongruous that this family scene should take place while I am interviewing one of the great minds of the twentieth century about a technology that is capable of changing the world of medicine.

Later, as things calmed down and the children disappeared for their naps and Karen and Ryan went to unpack, Bill and I got back down to the basics. I was to get used to the constant inter-ruptions of his life. If, before leaving Canada, I had half expected to hold these interviews in an office on the top floor of a com-mercial building, I was now under no such illusion. Life around Bill was a multi-layered, multi-faceted experience where holding onto a thread of thought was vital if one was to find a way back to a point of reference at a later date.

Bill leant forward to pour another cup of what was becoming an endless flow of green tea and said, "We are not always aware of the cause of a disease. It can be beneath the radar of our con-scious self. Sub-consciously, however, our body reacts to the subtle energetic changes in electrical bodies. The key to the QX is that it is the first energetic medicine device to test reac-tions where neither the patient nor the doctor knows what is being tested. In this way it is the unconscious reactions of the patient which are being detected by the computer, not the unconscious influence of the doctor, as is the case with point probes or Kinesiology."

This made a whole lot of sense to me, as the human interface always seems to be the weak link when a judgement of some kind needs to be made. We all have biases, things we believe or want to believe, and will often unconsciously skew findings to reflect the result we want to see.

"Now, let's take a look at the human body - how it works and what affects its efficient and disease-free operation. It is a complex organism with a constant flow of things we absorb and things we get rid of; these can influence our health positively or negatively."

"What do you mean by things?" I asked, surprised at this non-technical term.

"Well Simon, think about what goes into our body every day. We take in air, water, minerals, amino acids, fats, carbohydrates, thoughts, ideas, friendship, love, respect, mental stimulation, spiritual stimulation and a whole host of other nutrients. And many bad things, such as smoke, alcohol, pollution, additives and poisons. Then we detox our bodies by excreting urine, breath, stools, mucus, sweat, menses, bad feelings, fixations, addictions, coercions, intimidations, fetishes, manias, compulsions, spiritual doubts and a host of other excretions."

I screwed my face up as I tried to come to terms with the two lists. Bill looked at me and said, "You look confused."

"Well, I can understand air, water, food and stuff like that affecting our health, but what about the non-tangible items on the list, things like our feelings, fixations etc?"

"Think about it Simon. Surely you understand the negative influence stress can exert on the body, whether it's physical or mental?"

"Yes, I suppose, I just hadn't ever thought about it in these terms before, that's all."

"Well it's about time you did."

I was starting to realize that Bill expected me to keep up with him and that this wasn't going to be a simple case of recording a wealth of information and playing it back to my readers in reworked form. I would have to, at least in part, understand it. "So," I said, "life is a cycle of intake, chew, absorb or reject, assimilate, produce toxins, detox, and start anew."

"Well done Simon! Now you're starting to get it. If we now add the need to reproduce, our sexual needs enter the equation and we end up with a very complex cyclic flow of energies in and out."

All of a sudden I had this view of the human body as a massive machine that was exposed to, and influenced by, thousands of stressors, external and internal, physical, spiritual, societal and environmental. The complexity of it made my mind boggle.

I looked at Bill and said, "So, what you are saying is that when inward and outward flows are balanced a person is in health?"

"Precisely, Grasshopper."

"Is this what the QX does then?" I asked, noticing that I now felt comfortable enough to use the shortened acronym.

"Yes, but you need to understand more about the flow of disease before we discuss the device itself. Disease starts when a stressor or intrusion causes a disruption in the flow. The ease is now dis-ease." I nodded, urging him to go on as my brain cells started to make sense of all this.

"When a disease enters the body it sets off an alarm response as the body tries to deal with the stress the attack is causing. Symptoms are a sign of this alarm response. Allopathy... you know what this is Simon?"

"Yes, it's traditional medicine"

"Good, well allopathy treats the symptom. The allopathic medical doctor fights the symptom by trying to block some other flow. He uses anti-pyretics for fever, MAO inhibitors for depression, Serotonin uptake inhibitors for despair, calcium blackens for heart problems and antibiotics to attack the bacteria, thus weakening the immune system etc. So a child with a sore throat might have a toxin or nutritional deficiency as the deeper cause. The body is attempting to detox and stimulate the immune system with the symptom and trying to cure itself. Everything would be all right but if the child is taken to an allopath he or she targets the symptom straight away, and prescribes an antibiotic and an anti-inflammatory. What they have done, in effect, is thwarted the body's own attempt at healing, causing the disease to be driven deeper. Sure, the symptom goes away, but the cause lingers and another disease, perhaps more insidious than the first, continues to develop. This requires another allopathic remedy, and another, till the life force and the body's natural healing mechanism can no longer adapt and fight on its own. Now, degenerative disease clicks in and the downward spiral of disease-symptom-drug, disease-symptom-drug continues till death stops it. The average seventy year old is on eight drugs, the average eighty year-old on ten."

"Wow," was all I could utter. It made so much sense.

Bill was smiling; he saw that I was hooked. "Okay, now comes the real kicker Simon. As the stress continues the body goes into an adaptation phase and the symptoms go away due to familiarization and the disease progresses deeper. We now come to the all-important conclusion that must change the way we view medicine forever." He sat back in his chair and waited for a few seconds, letting the tension build before leaning forward and looking at me with his piercing blue eyes and saying, "Being symptom free is not a sign of health, in fact you can be symptom free and quite sick."

I let this revelation sink in for a few minutes and Bill seemed happy to let me be. He got up and walked to the refrigerator and rooted around for something to drink, settling eventually on a bottle of water. I noticed that his refrigerator was covered with plastic letters, children's drawings and photographs, the same jumble of family images we all have - was this what I expected of a quantum biologist? The implications of what he was saying were far reaching; after all, when we go to our friendly family doctor we expect him or her to give us something to provide some relief. Whenever we have a cold or flu we dose ourselves up with medications to suppress the symptoms. What Bill was saying was that we are also suppressing our immune system and driving the disease deeper.

"So Bill, are you saying that allopathy has no place in medical care?"

He sat down and said, "Not at all Simon. Allopathy has its place but it should be used for crisis intervention only."

"Let me continue explaining to you the dangerous cycle we enter into once the body starts to adapt to the disease and the symptoms disappear. After adaptation comes exhaustion, where the organs become weak; we then enter the functional phase where organs begin to function incorrectly, making too few or too many hormones, enzymes or whatever. The penultimate phase is organic, where the organ shrinks or grows - there is now physical disease. If the stressor continues, the last phase will occur which is death: cellular, organ system, organ, or death of the organism itself."

"Organism?" I queried.

"The body itself - the ultimate death."

"So, how would Nelson medicine treat me differently from the standard allopathic system?"

"Good question, Simon. We'll finish today's session with this, as I need to get on with some other work. We can reconvene here tomorrow and I'll tell you more about the Quantum Xrroid Conscious Interface itself."

I was both sad that the interview was coming to an end, but also exhausted at having the foundations of my albeit shaky belief in the health system so heartily rocked. Where did this leave me next time I was ill and what should I be doing to prevent the stressors from attacking my body in the first place?

"The flow of treatment works like this: firstly, we have to reduce or remove the cause of disease. This involves reducing the suppression or obstruction to cure, otherwise known as the SOC, which means getting the patient to take responsibility for their disease, their body, their mind and their spirit. Work can then begin on trying to repair damaged organs which have resulted from the disease."

"What about the flow we discussed earlier?" I asked.

"Absolutely, we have to open the flow of energy in the body using medical arts such as chiropracty and acupuncture. Then we can start to reduce the symptoms using natural methods including naturopathy. Once we have achieved all this we can deal with the constitutional make-up or lifestyle of the patient to identify how they can balance their life in a more positive way."

"So you do treat the symptoms; I was beginning to think that you didn't."

"Of course we want to relieve the symptoms, but it is not the primary concern: it is fourth on the list. Think about what we have discussed today and tomorrow you can ask all the questions you like, as we will be relating the Nelson Principles of Healing to how the QX device works. Now I must go and work with Franco on the software program."

I sat for a few moments, gathering my thoughts along with my tape recorder, laptop computer and sheaf of papers. I decided to walk to my hotel and think about what I had learned in what had turned out to be a long session with Bill.

Karen and Ryan came back into the kitchen saying they were sorry that they had been gone for so long but they had fallen asleep after unpacking. They asked me what I thought of Bill and I told them that he was an amazing person but sometimes difficult to follow. Karen nodded and said that he often had difficulty coming down to the average person's level and that he worked on a higher plain, which sometimes meant that he left out detail in his broad sweep approach. She explained that when he wrote he didn't care about typos or whether his grammar was correct. He feels that these things are insignificant and only small-minded people would get hung up on such things.

I started to understand my role here. Bill needed an interface between himself and his ideas and the general public, whether he realized and accepted it or not.

I suggested that we might meet for dinner that evening, but Karen and Ryan said that they had some catching up to do with Bill and that they would see me in the morning.

As I started to walk back to my hotel, along the cold and grey residential streets of Budapest on this February afternoon, I mulled over what Bill had told me. The one thing that stood out was the recurring theme that traditional medicine deals with symptoms more than it deals with cause. This confirmed what Ryan and Karen had told me back in Victoria and what Steve's research and my own had indicated. A lot of things were falling into place.

I reviewed Bill's stages of treatment and what became clear was that its naturopathic approach dealt with everything from behavioral medicine, psychology, homotoxicology, nutrition, allergy treatment to heredity factors. Only after it looks at all these factors does it look at re-growth and healing and then at dealing with energy blockages. Finally classical homeopathy deals with the symptoms.

So, none of this was weird, it couldn't by any stretch of imagination be thought of as 'beads and seeds' medicine, out in left field, or any other metaphor I could drum up. What had I been expecting, I asked myself, some sort of mumbo-jumbo snake oil? Far from it, this all made perfect sense.

I pulled the zip on my leather jacket up tight against my roll neck sweater and walked on. I thought about my own body and the lessons I had learned from my father. He always worked through illness, ignoring all the signs and symptoms of disease. Was this good or bad? On the one hand he was not hiding the symptoms by using medications, thus allowing his body's own immune system to deal with the disease. But on the other hand, was his body familiarizing itself with the symptoms and then ignoring them?

I had to acknowledge that my own body, both physically, mentally and spiritually was a mess. I work too hard, rarely rest and am wound tight as a coil spring most of the time. Spiritually I am searching for the unattainable - ultimate proof: proof that there is a God or proof that there is not. I'm a workaholic driving myself to what? An early grave or to some form of catharsis? Whichever comes first I suppose.

The closer I got to the city centre the more I left behind the shabby post-war apartment blocks, built under a sterile communist leadership which had little time for innovative design or quality. Bleak functionality was the order of the day and it was depressing. As the downtown core came closer however, the drab concrete blocks gave way to architectural beauty reminding me that once again so much in my life lately has been paradoxical.

At last I reached the hotel. I was starting to see some connection between Professor Nelson's philosophies, the traditional medical system and my own feelings about my body, mind and spirit. I wondered if by the end of this project I would have some answers or just a whole lot more questions.

Once I got to my room I decided to lie down and play back the day's interview in my head. An hour later I awoke, the sun had gone down and the room was dark. I was hungry and in need of comfort. I have travelled extensively on business around the world and always expect that the next time will be different, but it never is. Hotels are lonely places, period.

I decided to eat in the hotel dining room rather than wander the streets in the hope of finding a decent restaurant. The head waiter showed me to a table and as I waited for a menu I took in the old-world charm of the room. It was a white linen, tuxedos and best china type of place that reminded me of a top-class London restaurant circa 1950. There are still places in this world that seem to exist in a different era to the leading industrialized countries. They are a charming aberration in an otherwise increasingly sterile world. I looked around to see if I could see Miss Marples dining alone. She would, of course, be watching everyone surreptitiously and making notes. But she wasn't there, at least not in person.

My waiter returned and with a flourish handed me a burgundy menu wrapped with gold braid and its smaller brother, the wine list. Bread arrived and I started to relax. Hungarian bread is wonderful and this was as fresh as the selection at breakfast. I always think that half the pleasure of a meal away from home lies in the time available to peruse the menu and make one's choice. I decided to order wine first and take an hour or two to work my way through a bottle. As the food would undoubtedly be rich, spicy and heavy I settled on a 1997 Bikavér Barrique from the Szekszárd region. I called the waiter over and he seemed to approve of my choice. Within a few minutes I was gently swirling a full bodied ruby red wine around an enormous wine glass that would probably have suited brandy better. The wine had a warm bouquet of ripe tannin and tasted of dried fruit - I would need to choose a meal that would balance this assertive wine. After one glass I felt warm, secure, relaxed and happy.

My appetizer arrived as I was half way through my second glass: slices of roasted goose liver, served with a round of rice filled with garden peas and garnished with slivers of red pepper. It looked like a meal in itself and complemented the wine beautifully. The entrée arrived, Paprikás Csirke, chicken with a sour-cream paprika sauce served with cabbage rolls and caraway noodles. The wine and food were hearty to say the least and I virtually staggered back to my room. After several minutes channel-hopping I settled in to catch up with the news from Sky TV before dozing off in an alcohol and food induced coma.

I had a dream last night. A striking blond woman in her late for-ties came into my room and sat at the end of my bed. Her sheer magnetism forced me to pay attention as she explained that she was Desirée a close confidante of Bill's. She told me that she knew Bill better than anyone on earth, that she understood him. She looked very familiar, as if I already knew her. Desirée said that she had come to tell me about Bill, to give me an insight into him that I couldn't or wouldn't get from anyone else.

"At an early age," she began, "it was recognized that Bill Nelson possessed a special intellect. As a young child he demonstrated special mathematical and scientific skills. He maximized the Stanford Binet intelligence test and others at the age of eight, and thus it was reported in the local paper that his IQ was beyond measuring in the conventional system. He mastered calculus at age ten, Fourier conversions at age twelve, and Laplace transforms at thirteen."

Desirée stood up and walked to the dressing table opposite the bed and started looking through the drawers, appraising every item of clothing. I couldn't determine whether she approved or not. She seemed to be gathering her thoughts, before continuing in a low voice that seemed more Gloria Swanson than Marilyn Monroe.

"His performance in high school was astounding and record setting. He skipped grades in school and was allowed to attend college at night. Upon high school graduation he had already completed the first year of college. He got a perfect score of 800 on SAT math, physics, chemistry and biology. He attained a 34 on the ACT college test out of a possible 36 and was admitted to Mensa at the age of 16."

I felt as if I had dozed off because as I awoke from my dream within a dream Desirée was sitting in the armchair across from the bed with a Hennessy XO, rolling the glass between her hands in deep contemplation. She looked at me and said, "So you're awake again?" and smiled such a knowing smile that I felt as if she were looking inside my soul.

"Bill's exemplary performance led to his acceptance at many of the top colleges, including MIT, Cal Tech, Carnegie Melon and John Hopkins. However, he chose GMI where, out of five thousand applicants, he was chosen to work on the Apollo space project. His mathematical skills earned him the esteem and respect of his much older peers. He developed several patents and helped bring back the Apollo 13 astronauts. When they asked him to work on bombs and weapons, Bill's respect for the eightfold path prompted him to quit GMI. He went to several colleges but got his BSc and Masters at Youngstown State University. He published papers on ESP, reactivity, subliminal perception, brain physiology, NLP and mathematics."

Some of what Desirée was saying sounded familiar. I knew Bill had worked on the Apollo mission and that he had gone to Youngstown. I tried to wake myself up, or alternatively go back into a deep sleep, but the new reality of Desirée forced its way to the surface.

From a long way off her voice continued like a hypnotic stop-smoking tape.

"In 1977 he was hired to teach mathematics, para-psychology, meditation, mystic philosophy, and business math at Youngstown State University. On the day after his son, Daniel, was born, he taught his first class in mystic philosophy and ESP. Teaching allowed Bill to attend medical school at the NEO-COM consortium. When later he discovered that synthetic drugs were linked to his son's autism, he started to investigate seriously the power of natural medicine. When chemotherapy killed his grandmother Bill turned against the myopic purveyors of traditional medicine. His grandfather advised him never to compromise and to always be steadfast in his beliefs of natural medicine."

Desirée stopped and became quiet. After a while she looked as if she had gone to sleep, her ample bosom rising and falling gently as it strained against her burgundy sequined cocktail dress. Then, just as I thought I too would seek sleep she started her tale again. "He left the medical internship and gave up any claims on a medical license. Guided by a determined heart, a superior intellect and gentle spirit, Bill set the course for the rest of his life: to bring awareness of the truth about medicine to people."

By this time I was getting quite used to my nocturnal visitor and decided to ask her a question. "Tell me more about his education and beliefs?" She smiled and flicked back her long blond waves, her fingers flashing red as they traced their way through her hair.

"He earned terminal degrees in naturopathy, acupuncture, law, counselling, homeopathy and medicine, which served to broaden his already deep scientific knowledge. His research into the split brain, comparative religions, mystic philosophy, ESP, and natural medicine led to a very extensive and comprehensive background. As if all this was not enough, he attended a seminary in 1972 for religious education. During this time God spoke to him and told him to rewrite molecular biology. He took this message very seriously and spent the next ten years writing the Promorpheus Treatise. In 1982 he finished the work, copyrighted it and sent it to the Library of Congress. After almost twenty years it is still the most technical and mathematical treatise on life-process that exists. We have been nominated for the Noble Prize every year since."

This made me sit up, "We?" My apparition smiled and said, "Yes, I am part of him and he is part of me - ying and yang." Before I could query this confusing turn of events she continued.

"In 1983 he developed a company, New Vistas Homeopathics, in Ohio. Later he moved it to Denver. Hundreds of homeopathics were developed, tested and researched by Bill and he became the one of the world's foremost homeopaths due to his phenomenal scientific and clinical understanding. Five patents in homeopathy, and several new technologies in Electrophysiological Reactivity later, and Xrroid technology was developed. The year was 1985. He registered the first electro-dermal device with the Federal Drug Administration in 1989 and developed the first interactive cybernetic loop medical treatment and diagnostic device. He lectured in over 50 countries all over the world, and his charismatic stimulating lecture style drew world-wide acclaim."

"What hasn't he done?" I ask.

"Well, not a lot, he has authored twelve books and over two hundred articles on homeopathy, electro-acupuncture, quantum biology and natural medicine. His QX software is the world's largest medical software package available today."

"But why are you telling me all this?"

"Because you are writing about him and his life and his work. And this can be dangerous. The dramatic technological gap between Bill and his competition makes intellectual comparison impossible. The competition cannot bear, or don't have the capability, to engage in cerebral discussion. So they most often resort to slander, bold faced lies, or innuendo. Mediocre minds, out of fear and trepidation, resort to lies, and there are many others that are only too willing to believe them. The competition will do most anything to stop comparison. Remember Simon, Albert Einstein once said: 'Great spirits get incredible resistance from mediocre minds.'"

" Desirée, I still don't know who you are and why you are here."

"I am here to help you see what few have the intelligence to recognize: Bill's most powerful skill is to blend the scientific analysis of the masculine left brain with the feminine intuitive skills of the right brain, and harmonize these apparently opposite philosophies in such a way so he can speak to each. This is one of Bill's greatest achievements and is the cause of hatred by extremists overly attached to their ideas. This path of discovery and technology has not been an easy one for Bill."

She smiled at me warmly as she picked up her long black chenille throw, and as she walked to the door, turned and said, "So, I suppose that's where I come in." I looked quizzically at her and she continued, "To touch your discretionary mind, relax your judgmental thoughts and open the right side of your brain."

I didn't see her leave; she just wasn't there anymore.

Next morning when I awoke I could have sworn there was a faint, but unmistakable, scent of Chanel No.5 in the room.

A WAKE-UP CALL

My name is Jackie. This is how the QXCI changed my son's life.

I raced to Sam's room, it was two in the morning and I could hear him moaning quietly and knew that he was suffering from another bad headache. Disabling and disorienting, they were getting progressively worse. Sam at 13 years old lacked the energy you expect to see in a teenager. He was also exceptionally negative in his outlook and suffered from mood swings over and above what any parent expects from an adolescent child. Our doctors had done some tests but found nothing conclusive; we were starting to get desperate. Then one evening after my netball practice, the conversation got round to health issues; our wing attack was talking about a new machine she had read about that diagnosed difficult illnesses. This device had received a double-page spread in a local magazine devoted to parenthood; the journalist had interviewed a mother and her daughter and the local practitioner who had treated the little girl. Heather, our goal defense and a close friend, leaned over to me and said, "Jackie, you should take Sam to see this woman, see if she can work out what's wrong with him - what have you got to lose?"

Several days later Sam had another attack which had him laid up for three days, white as a sheet and almost comatose. I decided that if traditional medicine couldn't help I owed it to my son to investigate alternatives. I dug out my old editions of the parent and child magazine my friend had mentioned and searched for the name of the practitioner that was featured. Before I could change my mind I made an appointment for Sam.

That was eighteen months and a lifetime ago. Our world has changed a whole lot since then. When we arrived Betina asked us to fill out a simple health questionnaire. She explained in detail what she would be doing and made Sam feel relaxed and comfortable as she hooked him up with wrist and armbands to what looked like a very ordinary grey box. For quite some time she worked at her computer as multiple screens came and went in a Technicolor jamboree. After a while she turned to face us and said that he had very high levels of candida in his system and gave us a homeopathic remedy. Looking closely at the screen the machine told her that he was allergic to corn and corn products and that he had had severe reactions to these foods. The computer screen showed several pages full of information, but she said that we should deal with just a few things at a time. Betina made some adjustments on the computer and said she was going to zap Sam with certain frequencies, which would help him. Sam thought this was great and asked if this was like that film where people were miniaturized and sent in a submarine-type vehicle into someone's body to seek out the bad cells. Betina laughed and said it was something like that; in fact, the reality was no less amazing and futuristic. Once the treatment period ended she sat down with us and told Sam that he had to take ownership of his illness and be responsible for curing himself by taking the homeopathic remedies she was going to recommend and by changing his diet.

As we left her practice, we looked at each other and said almost simultaneously, "That was weird!"

I was surprised that Sam bought in so readily to the regime Betina had given him. He cut out corn and corn products and changed his diet to reduce the levels of candida in his body. His symptoms, prior to visiting Betina, had been so severe that I think the poor child was willing to try anything. Later we would look back on those early days and realize that the way he took responsibility for his body was the turning point.

Over the next few weeks his energy levels returned to something like normal and his headaches stopped.

The whole experience was weird and I have difficulty in believing a little grey box and a computer could cure Sam so easily when traditional doctors couldn't. The reality is that Sam cured himself; the machine just identified what he needed to do. In this age of high technology our children's reality is multi-layered; fact and fiction rub shoulders as they search the Internet for homework answers and fight aliens on their X-Box's. Perhaps a machine telling Sam to change his diet was what he needed. Would he have listened if it been an old guy in a white coat telling him what to do? Who knows?

Myself, I'm a 40-something housewife; I didn't know whether traditional medicine or the QXCI really did the trick. Until, that is, sometime later when Sam fell off the wagon, started to eat the junk food again and started to feel lousy all over again. It was his idea to go back and see Betina; he said his body was telling him that he should smarten up and it needed fixing again. A wake-up call I suppose, for both of us.

The QXCI Explained

Over breakfast next morning I reflected on my nocturnal meeting with Desirée, who seemed, in the cold light of day, the feminine alter ego of Professor Nelson. From what I had heard so far about the QXCI device and the incredibly complicated software that was its interface, it had an uncanny ability to work on, and understand, the physicality and psyche of the feminine body and mind. As I chewed thoughtfully on a piece of caraway bread, I wondered why my subconscious mind had conjured up such a clear image of what a feminine Bill would look and act like.

I considered whether the device was really as good as it was made out to be. The philosophy behind it certainly seemed sound enough. Allopathy, that is your standard run of the mill traditional medicine, isn't working particularly well and in many cases is downright dangerous. Pharmaceutical companies pay out billions of dollars in settlement claims every year when their synthetic preparations deliver unexpected and often dangerous results, despite all their testing. Homeopathic and holistic medicine, on the other hand, is rarely the subject of litigation.

What I needed to find out was why more people didn't accept energetic medicine. In fact, sitting here in my hotel in Budapest, there was still the question of why I was still skeptical when I still believed that traditional medicine was very hit and miss at best and completely ineffective most of the time. I suppose it is a case of better the devil you know. From when we are small children it is ingrained in us that doctors know best. People have worshiped doctors as all-knowing and all-seeing prophets of our health. I can remember as a child having to dress up in my Sunday best to visit the doctor. My father worked in a factory, but if he needed to visit this paragon of virtue, knowledge and dispenser of wisdom, he would come home bathe, and put on his best suit. Whatever the doctor told him was treated as gospel and the drugs dispensed accepted like candy from a kindly but austere old uncle.

Energetic medicine has a hard job competing with this image. Even with friendly and professional complementary practitioners, one is still putting a whole lot of faith in the hands of a little grey box and a computer program that tells us health is our responsibility and that there is no quick fix in the form of a synthetic pill. When it comes down to a competition between cutting back on processed foods, paying for more expensive organic products, drinking a gallon of water a day and changing a generally unhealthy lifestyle, it's enough to make anyone say, 'just give me the pill!' We have all got used to the easy way out and look to ease our symptoms rather than deal with the real problem.

Too many of us live fast and furious lifestyles with little care for how we are treating our bodies. I know myself that my body is under stress: physically, mentally and spiritually. But attacking the problems and taking responsibility for them is a lot tougher than suppressing the symptoms. Bill was right yesterday when he said that the body goes into an adaptation phase where you get used to the symptoms. I harbor dozens of suppressed symptoms that I daily put on the shelf to deal with later. But later never comes, or comes too late. I am frightened, really frightened. I have managed to train my body to fuel itself with stress. I use adrenaline as a highly personal drug, one that no cop could ever find on me. One day, when the stimulation my body craves dries up and my body has no stress to feed it, what will happen?

I come back from these dark thoughts as the clink of plates and cutlery act like an alarm clock, pulling me back from that other space we inhabit when we put ourselves on autopilot. The few stragglers in the dining room are finishing their breakfasts and I wonder how many had made consciously healthy decisions about what they consumed, and how many like me were barreling through life as if it was a grand prix race where risk was just part of the game?

Once more it struck me that my personal situation was similar in many ways to how the health authorities and governments deal with delivering health services to their constituents. So many countries are failing to keep up with the health demands of an aging population, their systems becoming increasingly stressed. Instead of looking at root causes they feed the stress with increasing amounts of money, which they can ill afford. The system gets addicted to cash, which it needs in progressively larger quantities. Each dose has less effect than its predecessor, until the whole thing collapses, imploding on itself as it struggles to find relevance in a strange new world.

Later today I hope to learn more about the QX and how it works. I wish I had paid more attention to Joe Sedgewick in my physics classes all those years ago, a wonderfully bizarre teacher. My favorite memory of him is of a huge fart that he recorded in the middle of taped music, which was to be played as a background for parents viewing their children's science projects during the school open house. As the music played continuously in a loop, we waited patiently for the explosive movement to see if anyone would cotton on. Parents engrossed in their offspring's projects, were seen to jerk their heads up at the sound of the offending noise only to shake their heads in doubt as the moment passed and Mozart's string concerto continued, as if nothing had happened. The scientific importance of this caper eludes me, but it taught me that not all adults, and certainly not all teachers, conform. I met Joe again for the first time in 35 years some time ago and he hadn't changed a bit. It wasn't long before he was telling me about his morning's masturbatory episode all the while looking for any sign that he might have managed to shock me. He may have been an old man by then but the twinkle in his eye as he reached to shake my hand after telling me this was just like it was all those years ago in chemistry class. Bill would undoubtedly have liked Joe. Desirée would have loved him.

It seems to me that there is a great need to educate the public about energetic medicine. It needs a human face; its mysteries need to be uncovered. Energetic medicine is a bit like a black hole; invisible and only detectable by the effect it has on the world around it. Perhaps, if I write a book about Bill's marvellous device, I can help make it accessible to all the people who otherwise might never give it a chance.

Back at Bill's apartment, lunch is being served and huge dishes of vegetarian lasagne and green salad are taking up most of the table. I take the opportunity as we eat to sit back, metaphorically speaking that is, and listen to the various conversations going on around the table between Bill, Karen, Ryan, Ildiko, Bill's adult son Daniel and the various staff members bringing food in and out of the room. The whole is a wonderful mix where the line between staff and family blurs into insignificance.

The primary topic is the party everyone attended last night. I had been invited but had declined. It was held in a private nightclub housed deep in the bowels of a nearby building. I had been given a tour of the establishment on my first day and found myself suffering from something akin to claustrophobia. It wasn't so much the closed-in space, but being underground and having to walk through tunnels to get to the main club area, which had low brick ceilings and brick walls. The musty smell unique to cellars was pervasive, although much had been done to spruce the place up. I have never been inclined to take up 'pot-holing' or as the Americans call it, spelunking.

The idea of spending time in close consort with a large number of people in what looked for all the world like an abandoned Hungarian resistance hideout filled me with dread. Apparently several local transvestites were guests and treated everyone to some highly professional cabaret acts. It appeared that I had missed quite a night and I was starting to feel a little left out. Perhaps my conservative nature and underground fears were holding me back once more from experiencing real life.

I started as I heard Desirée's name mentioned. Ryan was saying how Desirée was the star of the show. A shiver ran up my spine and I could feel the hairs on the back of my neck stick up. My mother always told me that this happened when someone was walking over my grave. As he described this glamorous and charismatic woman who had danced and sung on stage, I could see my apparition from the previous night, my guide to understanding Bill.

Karen looked at me and said, "Simon, are you okay? You look very pale - are you feeling alright?"

"No, I'm fine," I spluttered. "Probably just a bit tired, jet lag, lack of sleep, just the usual."

Ryan continued, "The dancer with the Python, now she was great...." He carried on reliving the gyrations of snake and dancer and I caught only bits of the story as I considered the coincidence of Desirée, the cabaret star and Desirée, the confidante. "...and when she put the snake down Franco's pants well..."

Karen's voice broke into my thoughts. "We need to get you onto the QX Simon, see what we can do about your sleeping; I'm worried about you."

Bill turned to me and said, "Yes, you must look after yourself, you need sleep, the body needs time to restore and renew itself, time to heal. You're out of balance, it's obvious."

If only he could see inside me I thought; he would be shocked at the wreckage that makes up Simon Alder's physical and mental state. It's not that I'm addled with disease or anything, or not to my knowledge anyway, it's just that I know everything is out of balance and struggling to work well. I realized at that moment that I was concerned, perhaps even frightened that the device, Bill's machine, could do just that - assess me like a garage mechanic checks out a high performance car, reducing me to a bunch of energetic impulses and discovering all my hidden secrets.

"Bill," I countered, trying to deflect attention away from my potential health issues, "tell me how the QX works, and please try to keep it as basic as you can."

"Yes," Ryan said enthusiastically. "I've read all the material and have used the device myself, but would love to hear from you Bill as to how it actually works."

"The QX medical device," Bill began, "is a biofeedback TENS device. It is designed to stimulate conscious awareness of our unconscious processes."

"Our unconscious processes?" I questioned.

"Our unconscious is always aware of the initial interference in flow," Ryan chipped in.

"Exactly!" Bill nodded at Ryan, recognizing that this young man had done his homework while, I felt sure, casting a surreptitious glance in my direction. Stupidly, I felt the need to compete and earn the approval of the master.

"So the way a patient starts the healing process is by the QX interfacing with his or her unconscious awareness. But how?" I asked.

"Using the TENS capacity of the QX, we can use a cybernetic loop to deal with the causes of the disease. The device actually zaps pathogens and shows up nutritional problems. It stimulates repair of injuries, helps with detoxification, desensitizes allergies, reduces stress and a whole lot more."

Ryan then broke in, talking about how the QXCI's best use was in releasing blockages in flow. I still didn't understand a whole lot of what was being said, but at least the language was becoming familiar.

"I thought it used acupuncture." I blurted out, caring less about looking a fool than leaving without a full understanding of something that seemed to defy understanding.

Bill reached forward and picked at the salad and I noticed what beautiful hands he had, his fingernails were manicured and shiny, radiant in health. "The QX detects faults in the acupuncture meridian flow and corrects them. It can also find faults in the energetic make-up and correct them too. It can even find faults in brain-waves and correct them." He licked his fingers one by one. "Finally, the system helps to find ways of reducing symptoms through other naturopathic means."

I started to see the direct link between his principles of healing and the way the device operated. I wondered where the man stopped and the machine started.

"So, the primary goal of our system is to stimulate the body to heal itself."

The tape recorder clicked loudly and everyone around the table took it as a signal to stretch and wander off to the washroom or get a drink.

Karen started to make more green tea. I was becoming hooked on the stuff; it was so much more refreshing than coffee, which is the worshiped brew on the West Coast of Canada. Kareem came into the kitchen and asked if I needed a ride to my hotel later. I nodded. Everyone was so hospitable and I found myself regretting my decision to move out of Bill's place. Once more I cursed my inability to deal with unfamiliarity and non-conformist atmospheres; questioning what really made me uncomfortable enough to leave.

Bill excused himself saying that he had to deal with some issues relating to the software with Franco, whose team was still plowing their way through sheaves of notes relating to what the new upgrade should contain. As he disappeared into the dining room he suggested re-convening in an hour or so.

Kristy appeared and asked whether anyone had shown me the film studio and Bill's new penthouse suite that was under construction. I happily took the tour and came back with several new pieces to the enigma that was Professor Nelson.

"Tell me Bill," I asked once we were all back round the table, "where did it all start? What made you get into energetic medicine?"

"Well, I always wanted to work with people and I became interested in medicine. But I realized that the philosophy of traditional medicine was based entirely on chemistry. It looked at the chemistry of the body through blood and other ways, and treated it with more chemistry, even worse, synthetic chemistry - drugs!"

I nodded but said nothing, hoping that the flow of information would continue.

"Then I came across work being carried out by the Germans on energetic medicine and discovered that they were measuring the electrical nature of acupuncture points and the electric potentials of the body. My research showed that although lots of people were studying the electrical nature of the body, not a lot of progress was being made. Once again the problem was that all the work was centered around chemistry."

"So Bill, your interest was more in the area of electrical energy?"

"Yes Simon, my background was as an electrical engineer so I wanted to be able to measure voltage, capacitants, inductants, susceptants etc. I wanted to look at the human body as if it were a television set."

"A television set?" Karen broke in laughing, "You'd make a great TV repair man Bill."

Bill was not going to be deterred, I could see by the glint in his eyes that we were covering ground that stirred him up and got his juices going. "I would! A repairman will measure the entire electrical parameters of a television set and find out where the problems are and bring the picture into focus. In the body we can do the same thing, we can discover where the disease patterns are and if necessary break up the patterns or alternately stimulate or enhance them."

Ryan chipped in, "But what I don't understand is why weren't other scientists taking this non-chemical route?"

"Think about it Ryan. Research funding was coming from the pharmaceutical companies; discovering how to treat disease with electrical energy was not something they wanted to fund. They wanted to fund something that would lead to the manufacture and sale of synthetic drugs."

Ryan asked something else, but my mind was retracing discussions with Steve around the research he had carried out on pharmaceutical companies and the huge amount of money they spent on developing drugs, advertising them and convincing doctors to prescribe them.

"...a bit creepy though isn't it? It reminds me of electric shock treatments and all that stuff." The conversation drifted back into my consciousness.

"No, no, no." Bill said. " But in my early days I did measure people's brain-waves and their patterns by basically taking a voltage reading. I also measured heart rhythms using an electro-cardiogram to measure their amperage."

"What's an electro-cardiogram when it's at home?" I asked.

"I'm glad you asked." Bill said. "It is a timed recording of the electrical impulses generated by depolarization and repolarization of myocardial cells during a cardiac cycle." Seeing blank looks around the table he continued, "Basically, following electrical stimulation of muscle cells there is a change in the electrical potential, which the ECG measures using a galvanometer." Bill smiled broadly, and I got the distinct impression he was in his element, dragging us along behind him and taking no prisoners in the process.

"The last thing I measured was skin resistance."

"Okay," I intervened. "So you measured brain waves; what did it tell you?"

"Well I got two people who were in a long-term committed relationship. People, who knew each other well, loved each other, people who were very close. We isolated them in two different buildings and put one of them in a darkened room and exposed them to intermittent flashes using a high-intensity stroboscope over a two-hour period."

He stopped for a few seconds to allow us to absorb and visualize this scenario. "During this time their partner had their brainwaves, heart-rate and skin resistance measured. We then asked the person to guess when their partner was being exposed to these blasts of light. It turned out that their guesses were nearly always wrong, in fact lower than what one would expect from random chance guesses. What was surprising though was that their body electric, as measured through their brain, heart and skin reactance, told a different story: these subconsciously reacted to the stimulation being received by their loved one."

"Wow" said Ryan. He could have taken the words right out of my mouth.

"So, that was when I started to get really interested in how the body reacts to different things even through remote stimulation."

I felt that I had just been privileged to see the birth throws of the QXCI, those early influences that set Bill on his chosen path. Who could have known that it would have led to such a complex scientific and medical miracle?

Over the next couple of hours Bill explained how the next twenty years saw him measuring acupuncture points and studying brain-wave functions and becoming increasingly involved in the technological side of it. It was not until 1985 that he registered his first device with the Federal Drug Administration. This early device diagnosed the body electric of a person, measuring 10 different functions every millisecond. I recalled that the new QXCI measured 55 different functions every millionth of a second. It wasn't until 1990 that he registered a device that would deliver therapy.

As he stopped for a few seconds to consider what to say next, my mind recalled the research I had carried out prior to coming to Budapest and the many conversations with Karen and Ryan. Professor Nelson had got into initial difficulty with the U.S. authorities in the form of the Federal Drug Administration when he put both diagnosis and therapy into one computer program so that one device could both identify health problems and then treat the patient as well. They refused to register this amazing new medical miracle but would give no reason why.

In 1992 Bill arrived in Budapest to discover that the Hungarian authorities had no such hang-ups and welcomed him with open arms. They immediately saw the potential of the device for reducing the amount of expensive pharmaceuticals used. In poor economies people have a difficult time paying for prescription drugs for things like epilepsy and depression, for instance. So-called wonder drugs, such as Prozac, were out of the reach of the average person. A drugless therapy offered new hope. Bill's discussions with the Hungarian authorities were a lot more open than with their counterparts in the United States and they saw the potential for curing depression, Alzheimer's, epilepsy and a wide range of other electrical functions in the body. They opened their minds and accepted the fact that a medical biofeedback device could detect bad patterns and correct them, something the FDA couldn't or wouldn't do. It was at this time and in this environment that the Professor was able to develop a cybernetic loop that was able to detect these irregular electrical patterns, disease patterns if you like, and correct them via the power of the computer at biological speeds. This all led to the QXCI being registered in Europe and imported into the United States and Canada. The support and succor Professor Nelson could not get in his home country was offered wholeheartedly by his new Eastern European allies.

The key thing I now wanted to know was how the device could distinguish between the electrical signature of healthy organs or tissue and that which was diseased.

"Bill, how does the QX read the electrical signatures of all parts of the body, identifying one part from the other? And are you saying that every part of the body has a different current, a different wavelength? Is it like tuning a radio looking for different frequencies?"

"Okay Simon, think about the cells that are, say, in your little fingernail and in your nose. They have the same DNA yes?"

"Well yes, of course they do."

"But the question is how do the cells in the fingernail know how to make a little fingernail and the cells in the nose know how to make a nose?"

Karen chimed up, "Because they are different electrically?"

"Good Karen, yes, because they are in a different electrical field. If we were to transplant them they would take on the characteristics of their new location. This is why plastic surgeons can take tissue from one place and transplant it in another and it will eventually take on the characteristics of its new home. The key thing is that the smaller the amount of tissue transplanted the more successful and stronger the organism will be. To sum up, the DNA may be identical, but the energy field is different."

"So basically, that's how the QX works: it can read and understand subtle energy imbalances in the body and actually correct them...Wow. But I still don't understand how it can tell all the different electrical signals apart, you know good from bad - doesn't one signal drown out another? Isn't it like a radio receiving too many signals one on top of another and resulting in a whole lot of white noise?"

I was on a roll. Before Bill could answer I said, "So, if I have a fungus somewhere in my body that is going to harm me, your device can somehow magically find the fungus and zap it? That's a tall order." I stopped abruptly, realizing that I had asked several questions without giving Bill a chance to get a word in.

Bill was smiling, a smile I was beginning to recognize, a smile that said that I was playing the game correctly and that he was enjoying himself. "What I have managed to do is measure the wave patterns of thousands of different funguses and I understand their electrical signature. Using the computer software and the device we can transmit the electrical signature to the patient and monitor how the patient reacts to it. The patient reacts to the fungus they have which is out of balance."

"Okay, I get it. Tell me more about the volts and stuff," I asked.

"Electricity is based on three major elements, volts, amperage and resistance. And if you can measure these three elements in an electrical circuit you will understand the circuit. In addition there are other elements such as capicitants, inductants, susceptants and reactants and all the other mathematical variants on volts, amperage and resistance."

"Okay, so some part of my body starts to act up, say my shoulder for instance. I have had a frozen shoulder for several months now. What would the QXCI do for that?" I challenged him.

"Well Simon, when something goes wrong it could be caused by a thousand different things. It could be due to some sort of trauma or infection, almost anything. What we would do is interfere with your system and cause a change in your electrical pattern to disturb the flow of electricity through the body."

"Isn't that what a chiropractor does," I asked.

"Precisely Simon! My we are starting to catch on aren't we?"

I shot him a look which was supposed to say 'get off my case,' but was probably more like a 'didn't I do well' smile. My god I need to harden up.

Not to be outdone Karen leant forward and said, "Yes, the chiropractor adjusts the spine say, to maximize the flow of energy through the spine and nerves thereby maximizing the health of the patient."

"But what we've developed with the QX goes way beyond that Simon, way beyond just purely chiropractic."

"Well I can see how your machine might assist in the flow of energy through the body. I've been to a chiropractor and felt the difference in energy for myself before and after manipulation. But what about mental disorders, surely the only way to treat them would be by using chemicals?"

Three sets of eyes darted toward me as Ryan, Karen and Bill looked in astonishment at the blasphemy I had just committed. I regretted it as soon as it was out of my mouth and remembered yet another truism my mother once told me: 'put your brain into gear before you open your mouth.' Will I never learn?

"Simon, Simon, Simon, I thought we had been through all that. The QX can assist in the treatment of almost any health problem, particularly mental ones. We have seen some wonderful successes in treating Alzheimer's disease, Parkinson's, autistic children and those with ADD. In fact we have seen people cured of Alzheimer's in one treatment."

"Wow, that's really futuristic medicine."

Ryan was once again showing his superior knowledge by suggesting that the device was registering optimal levels of electro-magnetic or bioelectrical waves.

Bill replied, "Well it does, but really it is the changes in the electrical field it measures after having first established a base line."

He continued, "Our bodies react to the energies around us. Every living organism has a reactive energy field that is in a constant state of flux. Our bodies are drawn toward nutrition while we repel toxins. When we are thirsty and in need of water our body is attracted to water. Once the therapist knows the standard baseline for your energetic state, he or she can identify whether you are in need of water or more oxygen for instance."

Bill was now looking at me in that patient way that said he knew I needed more explanation. "Simon, if you think of the human body as an electrical device you might understand it better. Basically, if we know what output an electrical device is supposed to put out, and we have a method of reading the output, we can easily see if it's doing what it should. If some outside source changes the output we can see it clearly and correct it. Clear?"

I nodded but I can't say it was completely clear. Each time Bill spoke I came up for air with a better understanding, but with more questions than before.

"Okay, Bill, so here I am a new patient and the QX needs to understand my baseline; how does it do it?"

He looked at me as if assessing whether I could handle a more in-depth explanation. He must have decided that his pupil was ready to go to the next level because he took a deep breath and launched into a detailed explanation of how the QXCI tested a patient.

"First of all the computer needs to develop a handshake with the patient to maximize the reactivity scores. It measures the trivector reactions of the patient to establish a link to the patient with resistance, voltage and amperage. In this way we create a connection for conductance, capacitance and inductance for magnetic, static and resistance link up."

"So what all this means Bill, is that your device, using the computer, creates an electrical relationship between itself and the patient, a two-way walkie-talkie system."

Bill raised his eyebrows, looked over his glasses at me and said, "If you like."

"Once the link is made," he continued, "the computer adjusts reaction timing, frequency interaction and the trivector interaction. This is what allows the device to auto-focus or adapt to the patient's needs automatically."

"Okay, I think I understand most of that, or at least I think I do, just don't test me," I said. "But what the devil is trivector interaction?

The next little while went by in somewhat of a blur, but he told me about the trivector pattern which is comprised of the three major co-factors of all electromagnetic phenomena which are amps volts, and resistance, or conductance, capacitance and inductance. Together they make a factor known as reactance. So far so good; he then went onto explain that electro physiological reactance (EPR) is a measurable factor in medicine that can indicate many aspects of the quality of a patient's health. What I found really interesting was that because EPR happens at the ionic rate this means that an EPR test can be done at centi-second speeds.

He told me that the advances in speeds of PCs and laptops has made a huge difference as they can now calculate the vast quantities of information involved in incredibly short periods of time.

I asked him to explain further how a test actually worked.

"In the calibration process of our EPR test Simon, we test the EPR of the patient to 20 samples of a low-reactive distilled water and several samples of toxic sugar, and insecticide, the highest known reactive substance. If the patient reacts to the toxic reactive materials significantly then the test can proceed. If the reactance is not significant then the computer will alter the test time or sensitivity till the calibration test is shown to be significant. Then the test can proceed. During the large QX test over 65 million bits of data are developed and analyzed; thus the need for a computer. At the end of the test the computer program can display the end results of 1.75 million bits of data done in the calibration of a single patient."

Karen and Ryan walked back into the kitchen and I realized that several hours had passed and we were still talking about how the QXCI worked. The complexity boggled the mind. The fact that one man had conceived and built it was beyond belief.

Karen said, "Have you told him what it's like from the patient's perspective Bill, or have you just been blinding him with science? What happens when a patient visits a practitioner Simon, is that they sit in a comfortable chair and fill out a basic form that asks them about their health in general. They are then hooked up to the device by a headband and arm and ankle bands. Bill's probably told you about the handshake which establishes the cybernetic loop. Once that's been done the practitioner can get a basic run down of the patient's health using the biofeedback/TENS program and the computer shows several screens that provide an overview of the patient's health and risk factors."

"What sort of things can it tell about a person?" I asked.

"Well, one of our practitioners working with a patient for the first time, reported that the device showed that she had undergone trauma to her head when she was only eighteen months old. When the patient checked with her mother she discovered she had fallen off the draining board while her mother had been washing her in the kitchen sink. Don't ask me why she was being washed in the kitchen sink. The point is that the woman had no idea this had happened, over thirty years ago, as her mother had never told her because she had always felt so guilty for dropping her."

Another chill travelled from the base of my neck down my spine, making me shudder involuntarily.

"The accuracy," Bill broke in, "is exceptional and enables the computer to provide a host of very precise health and wellness tips for both the therapist and the patient."

We were now getting into the real meat of how this device worked and I decided I would hold my questions and just listen. Karen and Ryan had quietly got up and indicated that they were going for a nap. I was getting tired too, but having got Bill in full flow I was not prepared to lose a moment of the great man's energy and time.

"Once the computer has measured the patient's electrical parameters the QX subjects the patient to minute electrical impulses and then monitors how the patient reacts in term of a scoring system. For instance Simon, you told us earlier that you are allergic to nuts and have some other allergies."

I nodded.

"The QX can test your reaction to over 300 potential allergens ranging from airborne and environmental allergens to food allergens. It can even tell you that your body does not tolerate a particular food that in your everyday life has no noticeable effect on you, but which in reality is not good for your system and is affecting your energy flow. The computer lists all allergens and provides the therapist with a colour coded table with the more serious offenders highlighted. Removing some of the foods from your diet, which show high readings, can have a major benefit to your well-being."

"How experienced do practitioners or therapists have to be then Bill?" I asked.

"That's one of the benefits of the QX Simon. It has several automatic treatments which mean that the system interacts with the patient, evaluates the progress it is making and terminates automatically whatever program it is running when it has accomplished its goals. If required, it can prolong or intensify the treatment."

"So is it the patient who is controlling the treatment?" I asked.

"Exactly, no longer do we have external forces imposing themselves on the patient's body; the body itself has a say in what is happening to it."

Bill caught me in a yawn and suggested we break off and recommence tomorrow. Part of me wanted to continue because we were mining such a rich seam, but I knew I wasn't concentrating well and needed time to regroup. I decided to walk back to my hotel as it was still light and I needed the cold air to wake me up and clear my head. The walk would give me time to think. I said my goodbyes and headed out.

As I struck out along Bákóczi ut I considered the fact that Bill's incredible knowledge of quantum physics, quantum biology and the human body gave him a totally unique perspective on the world of medicine. Where traditional doctors and pharmaceutical companies worked in the world of chemistry, he worked in the world of electrical energy. They were two completely different routes to the same place using two completely different maps. I could see why the pharmaceutical companies, or as I saw them called in the John LeCarre novel The Constant Gardener, 'pharmas', would prefer and protect their chemical route. Attacking the problem with cocktails of chemicals allows them to concoct hundreds of thousands of preparations, which can then be distributed through a network of willing dealers to unsuspecting customers. I suppose they are not called drugs for nothing.

I recalled a conversation with Steve, my research sidekick back home, who told me that over $78 billion worth of prescription and over-the-counter drugs are produced each year in the United States alone. What amazed me at the time was that he showed me a survey carried out by a group called the Substance Abuse and Mental Health Service Administration (SAMHSA), which showed that over 20 million people in the United States, over the age of 12, have used one or more psychotherapeutic drug some time in their lives.

On my long journey to Hungary I had reviewed the many pages of research Steve had prepared for me and now started to think about the world of chemicals and medicine. I was so engrossed in my thoughts that as I stepped off the curb a taxi clipped my brief-case, waking me out of my self-induced trance. The cab's horn blasts faded quickly as the vehicle screamed off and I considered how cab drivers seem to be the same the world over: you could plonk them down in any city in the world and they would be at home within hours.

Back to my mental review; I thought to myself how massive and highly profitable the pharmaceutical industry really is. We all know it's big, but still it's surprising to discover how big and how powerful it really is. I remember on the plane looking at an article published in the British Guardian newspaper recently, which stated that not so long ago drug companies profits were merely the size of a nation's GDP, but now, after some major mergers, they are larger than that of a continent. In fact, it went on to say that, the combined worth of the world's top five drug companies was twice the combined gross national product of all sub-Saharan Africa. And their influence on world trade was even stronger.

Surprisingly we are going through a period where less new drugs are being developed. The reason? Pharmas can make more profit by selling existing drugs to new markets. The hype is astounding as they turn their attentions increasingly to 'lifestyle' drugs which treat things like erectile dysfunction, obesity and bald-ness. They then create markets for them by throwing millions of dollars into advertising campaigns. Since drug companies started advertising on television in the early 1990s, sales of prescription drugs have almost doubled.

Television is not the only vehicle to assist in this increase; doctor visits by sales representatives of the pharmas have increased dramatically over the last ten years or so. One key question I'd like to ask them is, 'who's paying for the mega bucks being spent on these massive ad campaigns?' You can bet your bottom dollar that's the reason behind the increasing cost of all drugs, not only the new ones where the excuse for high prices has always been the cost of research, but the old staples too. Steve's big fear, which he sat down one night back in Canada to explain to me, is that if it is true that the drug companies are more about profit than health, then we can expect them to start spending more research dollars on the new lifestyle, designer drugs that are aimed at the wealthy rather than drugs to eradicate AIDS in Africa where patients have little or no money. Steve's research, using a great web site called U.S. Business Reporter, showed that American pharmas enjoy staggering gross profit margins of between 70-80 percent, and with prices rising faster than inflation this is only going to get better, or worse, depending on your point of view.

I let this thought sink in for a few minutes as I continued my walk. Once again, I noticed that the closer I got to the city centre the better condition the housing was in; the architecture was changing to reveal more historic buildings such as the Hungarian National Museum just north of Kálvin tér.

Talking with Bill made me realize that there is another way to help people, a non-chemical way. But I needed to know more about the difference between the two. I decided that tomorrow I would ask him to explain how electrical treatment and chemical treatment were interrelated.

With my hotel in sight my thoughts turned away from the QXCI and toward home comforts, or at least hotel comforts. I thought about Canada and the great sense of security familiarity gives one. I also thought of my children back at home and started to feel homesick. At times like this, so far away, I should have been missing my wife, but it just made me wonder whether we had a future at all. Our relationship has been coasting for many years, waiting for the kids to grow up and leave home. Once they leave will there be anything left to hold us together? I doubt it.

My hotel room was stuffy and overheated, as so many hotels are. I kicked off my shoes, opened the window to its fullest (which is severely limited in order to deter suicidal individuals and adventurous children), lay on the bed and almost immediately fell asleep.

Next morning I awoke early after another fitful night.

At breakfast I met a neurologist named Phillip who was visiting Budapest from England. He was in the city to meet with some colleagues at the Institute of Experimental Science. The institute, he told me, specializes in biomedical research, particularly in the field of neuroscience. He mentioned that Hungary was very open to new ideas and that he also wanted to visit the offices of the International Medical University of Natural Education run by someone called Professor William Nelson. He explained that it was an internationally accredited correspondence university offering some fascinating courses on quantum biology. I explained that I was currently working with Professor Nelson, and then we had that whole 'it's a small world' discussion.

Once Phillip left, I sat for a while drinking my coffee and pondering how synchronicity was becoming such a part of my life, although people tell me that coincidence is not as uncommon or as unlikely as we think. Apparently if you sit next to a stranger on a plane, 99 times out of 100, two or fewer intermediaries will link you to that person. Apparently the absence of coincidences would be the most incredible coincidence of all. By this time my head was spinning, probably from too much coffee, so I decided to get myself out and about and take up with Bill where we left off yesterday.

I turned up at Bill's place to find it a hive of activity with breakfast still in full swing. The children were running around like freshly charged Energizer bunnies and Ildiko was playing some sort of game with them that resulted in green alien slime being deposited on the ceiling. As it hung there defying gravity, I wondered if and when it would decide to give up its tenuous hold on reality and fall to earth, or in this case, quite possibly my head.

Eventually the morning chat of planning the day, the meals, who was arriving, who was leaving, which staff member was doing what and when, petered to a natural close. Bill and I were left once again to finish my heroic journey of understanding. Just as we began Karen and Ryan came in, fresh green tea was made and the serious work was sidelined while we caught up with their activities.

Some time later I managed to ask my question about the inter-relationship between chemistry and electricity as it applies to medicine and the human body.

"Simon, let's help you to understand this once and for all. The QX measures electrical fields within the body, Okay?"

I nodded.

"We believe, here at the Maitreya Institute, that it is electrical fields that produce chemical changes in the body. When someone gets sick it is their electrical functions that are the problem."

"Like a short circuit" I said.

"More like a blockage in their energy flow," chimed Karen while she poured boiling water onto the omnipresent green tea."

"Yes," said Bill, "this blockage can be at an acupuncture point or in a vertebrae of the spine. The QX identifies the problem and stimulates the flow of energy by removing the blockage."

"It's all a matter of focusing the body rather than doing something drastic like swallowing loads of pills," Ryan said.

"What makes the body's energy flows get disrupted and out of whack?" I asked, with my normal grasp of technical language.

Karen, back at the table and pouring tea, said, "It can be lots of things Simon, perhaps the body is suffering from some kind of stress, is infected with parasites, lacks the correct nutrition or has been exposed to some toxins."

"What the practitioner does, with the help of the QX device, is to locate energy blockages and fix them at what we call biological speeds, of thousands of a second. This Simon...," Bill continued, "is a whole new form of medicine."

"Parasites?" I said screwing my face up.

"Yes,' said Karen. "We all have various parasites living in our body and many of them are harmful. The QX can identify them and kill them."

"The device actually zaps them with an electrical current?"

"Well, basically yes - in the same way it deals with viruses."

Bill broke in, "Simon, I don't want you to go way thinking that the QX is a total cure-all. I've heard you use the term 'Star Trek medicine' and to many people, because it is out of the realm of their understanding, they think it is science fiction, but in reality it is a tool like any other. Patients have to do a lot themselves. It starts with them taking responsibility for their bodies and, if necessary, adopting a healthier lifestyle. So practitioners using the QX need to teach their patients to be healthy. The device doesn't cure everything all the time, practitioners will use homeopathic preparations and diet and a host of other things in tandem with the device itself."

I felt that I needed to ask the ultimate question at this stage, "Can it detect and cure cancer?" I asked.

Bill took a deep breath, "The device tells us of the probability of cancer. It does not have the capability of diagnosing cancer with 100 percent reliability, but it can detect a high probability. In this case the patient may be sent for an MRI or blood work to try to identify whether cancer exists. At the same time the practitioner would be discussing their general health, including whether they smoke or experience high stress, all the time building a patient profile; basically giving them the works, a complete medical."

"How would you treat them?" I asked.

"By using natural medicines, not synthetic medicines. Nature's chemotherapy, not corporate scientist's chemotherapy."

By this time things were starting to come into focus for me too. I was at the birth of a completely new type of medicine. Even though Bill had been working on this for over twenty years it was still new. I wondered how long it would be before the general public and those people and businesses with vested interests would start to accept it for what it had to offer. It was obvious the public would lead the way, with industries such as pharmaceuticals only accepting it kicking and screaming, unless of course they found a way to make money out of it, in which case they would be at the vanguard of this new opportunity to heal.

"I want you to go and talk to some of the practitioners that use my device Simon. I want you to see it through their eyes and through the eyes of their patients."

The next day I was to head home, but that evening my friends Karen and Ryan took me to dinner. We met at my hotel and they brought along Destiny, their youngest child. We talked about their website which they use to promote the QXCI, while they travel the world like missionaries, educating people on the benefits of the machine, demonstrating its miracles and turning skeptics into believers at every turn. I wondered when I would see them again. They were still going through the immigration process which would allow them to relocate to Canada but this was turning out to be a lengthy and unnecessarily bureaucratic process. We discussed the book, the very thought of which frightened me. I had told Bill that I could write it in six or seven months, but the more I thought of the complexity of the device itself and the politics surrounding it, the more doubts crept in. We said our goodbyes and hugged for what seemed like an age. Eventually they left.

Back in my room I felt lonelier and more exposed than I had ever felt before. I slept poorly but that was nothing new. As I checked out of the hotel before dawn I reflected on my few days in Budapest: it felt as if I had been in Hungary for weeks.

Kareem turned up a little early to take me to the airport. He had his cousin with him. I was pleased to see him and glad he continued to prove reliable. On the way to Ferihegy I remembered the journey from the airport to Bill's apartment just a few days before, the fears I had, the uncertainty, and reflected on how much I had changed in such a few days. I looked across at Kareem and smiled inwardly; I had grown to like this man for the support he had given me, and the fact that he was always there when I needed him. I could see why Bill and Ildiko relied on him so much. Kareem, with cousin in tow, carried my bags into the airport and stayed with me while I changed my tickets, as I had decided to break my journey home with a stopover in England. When the time came to go airside I handed Kareem all my forints. I knew it was a fair bit of cash in Hungarian terms, but I felt he deserved it. Characteristically he tried to refuse it but I insisted and got my reward via a broad smile and a clap on the back. I hoped I would get a chance to meet him again sometime.

QXCI: ANOTHER WAY

My name is Vicky, this is how my son fought ADD and won.

"I know it sounds like quackery but all I know is that it worked for my friend."

J ill was obviously uncomfortable telling me about this space age machine. She works in a government office and is probably the most reserved person I know, so I took what she had to say seriously. I had been telling her about Brent, my 16-year-old son. He had been suffering from depression and I was worried about him - it is so unlike him to be down. She gave me the number of a lady whose child had experienced similar problems. I called her and she gave me the information I needed - an alternative health practitioner who could help. Her name was Penny.

I'm an X-Ray technician at the local hospital. The change in Brent was gradual, so gradual that I really didn't realize it was happening. Oh sure, I knew that he was down sometimes, and that he occasionally lost his temper over little things, but I put it all down to hormonal changes - the teenage years and all that. We got through the terrible twos and a few other tense times along the way, but it all evened out in the end - he's a good kid.

But as the months went by he didn't grow out of it, in fact, it got progressively worse until he was profoundly sad, a shadow of his normal self. His schoolwork suffered, not that he had ever shone academically - he had always found school tough. His few friends seemed to drift away, his cell phone would ring less frequently and he would spend increasing amounts of time lying on the sofa watching television or playing video games. I think he was drinking heavily at the few parties he did attend - or so we heard from other parents.

I asked him once, when we sat quietly together one afternoon, how he felt and he said, "I'm sad, but I don't know why - I don't want to be but I am."

That was when I decided we needed help and went to see our doctor. He referred us to a psychiatrist, but neither Brent nor I warmed to him. His receptionist called a few times saying that it was important that we keep going to him, but Brent didn't want to go back, so we didn't. We tried lots of other avenues, I researched depression on the Internet, went and saw family services, visited other specialists, but nothing seemed to help.

I got really frightened about Brent's behavior. He couldn't get to sleep at night and then we couldn't get him up in the morning. Simple tasks became increasingly difficult for him to focus on. He was suffering; it was like something was eating away at him from the inside - taking his willpower.

Doctors had said that they thought it was, at least in part, attention deficit disorder, although they never seemed sure. We saw a specialist who worked with children suffering from attention deficit disorder and attention deficit hyperactive disorder, which are basically the same thing. He believed that many of his patients had high levels of parasites in their bodies and he was researching whether there was a connection. He did some blood work on Brent, which went down to the States for special testing. The results were positive, but our own doctor refused to believe that Brent had parasites because he was not suffering from stomach problems.

All the time Brent continued to sink lower and lower. It was then that Jill suggested we seek something different, a new kind of therapy, a new approach.

The first session with Penny amazed me; the machine knew so much about Brent, more than even Brent knew. Within just a few minutes Penny said, "Wow, this young man has really low dopamine levels; no wonder he's not doing very well." It was the first time I felt some relief - just knowing that something had shown up, that it wasn't all in our minds. Penny looked at me and said, "I can help him with this." She told Brent that the QXCI would zap him. Now, she was really talking Brent's language, and he smiled - a rarity at the time.

The thing that surprised me the most was how ordinary it all was. Penny is as far away as anyone could be from an evangelical preacher, faith healer or saviour. She is just a pleasant woman working out of a renovated home basement. Professional but no pretensions, she didn't even try to get us excited by the power of the machine; it was all very low key.

I have to admit, I was very skeptical. Let's face it: an ordinary woman, a grey box and a computer screen - how could she make a difference when all the doctors and specialists had achieved nothing? So I asked, "When could we expect to see a change in Brent?" I was expecting we would need numerous visits and thousand of dollars. "Oh," she said, "you'll see a change tonight." Yeh, I thought, and pigs might fly. She said that she had treated him for his lack of dopamine and also for worms and a number of parasites. There were those parasites again, the ones our doctor didn't believe existed.

On the way home I asked Brent how he felt and he said, "Drowsy, Mom, drowsy." Great I thought, even lower energy than normal - just what I need. But then, as soon as we walked through the door my husband noticed it: there was something in Brent's eyes that hadn't been there for the longest time. They were bright, as if someone had turned on a light. It was like someone had given him a happy pill. Later we asked him how he felt and he said, "Well, on the way home I felt kinda like sleepy, but okay sleepy, then when I got home I felt different, sort of alive for the first time.

It's kinda' hard to describe, but it was like taking a journey from somewhere awful to somewhere wonderful, but like really quickly. It's cool, really cool."

Later we questioned him a little more about his experience with the QXCI and he said, "At first I wasn't sure; it was sort of boring, but the wrist, ankle and headbands and the computer program were interesting." Full of contradictions, our Brent. He went on, "When I got home though it was like I was completely the opposite of how I used to feel." What he said next made me cry - tears of happiness, relief and joy at seeing my son back - he said, "All the happiness I couldn't express before came flooding back."

We are still in shock, the whole story sounds unbelievable, but whatever the QXCI did, it worked. And, the best thing was that it was all done without resorting to medication or any other invasive therapies.

Brent tells us that he feels a lot more positive and open-minded and that it all takes a lot of getting used to. For my husband and I, it has changed our lives. We are so much calmer - when you watch someone you love suffer day in and day out it wears you down.

As I walk along the street or through the park close to our house, I see people walking past and think to myself, how many of you are on medication, how many of you are suffering side-effects and taking one drug to counter another? The QXCI has shown us that there is another way.

Brent summed it up best when he said at dinner the other night, "Why doesn't everyone use the QXCI - it's so simple - no drugs - it's quick - it's painless and it knows, it really knows what's going on inside of you." He looked up and saw his Dad and me staring at him with beaming smiles on our faces as he took a third helping of lasagne.

"What? I'm a growing lad!"

HANNAH'S EPIPHANY

England

The time I spent with Judy and my experience with the QXCI device has given me a whole new perspective on why Simon chose me to carry out the research. He really annoys me sometimes with his agnosticism. If you start from a position of, "it is impossible to know," there is no way forward; you close all doors to the possible. And I know he is struggling with his position; I see chinks in his defense. He has a leaning toward reincarnation, he wants to believe in it - to a certain extent does believe, but can't make that final leap of faith. I am impressed though that he recognizes the need for balance in writing about the QX, especially as it provides me with work. The other evening I called to give him a progress report and we got into a fairly heavy philosophical discussion. The subject, as ever with Simon, was what can we really believe in? The conversation went something like this:

Simon: I can really only believe in myself, everything else could just be a dream. Descartes was right when he said: "I think, therefore I am."

Me: Ah, so you studied Descartes did you?

Simon: Well not studied exactly, but I know that he invented a method of systematic doubt and that he wouldn't believe in anything he didn't quite clearly see to be real.

Me: So how did he do this?

Simon: Basically, he would doubt everything until he got to a point where he could no longer see a reason to doubt it.

Me: But it is easy to doubt things. Didn't I read somewhere that he came up with the bright idea that demons could be presenting him with images of real things and therefore that was a reason for not believing in just about anything?

Simon: Well, yes, but you make him sound crazy. He realized that demons were highly unlikely, but the fact that they were possible, however remotely, was enough to cast a doubt on anything his senses perceived.

At this point, I was getting somewhat frustrated with both Simon and Descartes and the ridiculousness of the argument.

Me: But surely Simon, in that case the demon could be deceiving him about his own presence too!

Simon: Good point Hannah, but what you fail to see is that the fact that Descartes doubted at all, and had experiences, meant he must exist. If there was a demon deceiving him then he must exist for the demon to be able to deceive him. So in the end, the only thing he was really certain of was his own existence, which led him to utter those words immortalized a second time by the British pop group Bread: 'I think, therefore I am.' *Cogito, ergo sum.*

Me: Okay Simon, enough of the Latin. I'll go along with what you say, but it means that you have to give me this one point: according to all that you just said, Descartes showed that we can actually be more certain about the existence of subjective things than we can of objective things. Think about that Simon.

The line went quiet and I could almost hear Simon sucking on his teeth. It wasn't often I managed to stop him in his stride, but I knew he would go away and rehash the conversation until he could see his way through it. While I had his attention, I told him that my research was continually bringing up doubts about the QX, but they were being systematically overcome by patient and practitioner testimonials. I thought that capped the conversation quite nicely. I then reminded him that I was going to England the following week for my niece's wedding and he immediately gave me the names of a few practitioners to look up while I was there. Getting a vacation while working for Simon was obviously not going to be a possibility, that much was clear. I wondered if he ever took a break - and immediately doubted it.

England in August is pleasant - the rain is at least warm. I arrived at Heathrow airport and was greeted by my sister and her husband Stuart. Ninette is a strikingly beautiful woman: tall, long blond hair, Scandinavian to the nth degree and obviously my sister. She is fourteen years older than me, taller by an inch or so and a century more mature. I am never sure if I should be envious of her husband the lawyer, the Range Rover, the house in the country, two delightful grown-up children and of course Digby and Jasper, her two Golden Retrievers. She has everything wrapped up and secure: the perfect family, her future carefully planned and she is content. I have my freedom - I wonder if it is a fair trade?

We hug and kiss amidst a wheat field of blond hair being swept this way and that, by a mixture of air conditioning fans and people rushing past. Stuart takes me in his arms and kisses both cheeks and then holds me at arms length to take my measure. "Well Sis." Calling me Sis dates back to when he first dated Ninette. I was only nine. "You're looking great - Victoria must suit you." He grabs my bags and heads off to the car without waiting for a reply.

The rain is bouncing off the black road and forming individual, impossibly round, droplets on the Range Rover. I wonder fleetingly how many coats of Turtle wax Stuart has applied to get this effect. He's an all right guy, he wouldn't have been my choice as a life partner, but he's made Ninette happy and that's all that matters. She met him when she escaped the Prairies and came to England to study law. I remember when she left I felt she was deserting me, abandoning me to my one-dimensional parents and the one-dimensional town we lived in. I forgave her long ago. She never knew she was, at least in part, responsible for me moving toward things alternative, and some of them not at all healthy.

Ninette has two passions in her life, excluding her family. They are horses and gardening. Actually, make that three, I forgot Digby and Jasper. She rides most days, as befits a lady of leisure, and spends most of the spring and summer tending her extensive garden. She lives in Wokingham, Berkshire. Wokingham is a small, attractive town which reminds me of a magnificent oak tree being suffocated by ivy. It is only early in the morning that you can truly appreciate the ancient architecture and the market town aspect of Wokingham because by 9:30 a.m. it is heaving with traffic. To drive the half-mile or so of high street in rush hour can take about the same time as it would take me, back home, to drive the fifteen miles to Victoria, pick up some shopping, get home, make a pot of tea and drink it! I remember Ninette telling me that they often have to take a circuitous route around the town centre. This five-mile detour allows them to approach their house from the north and thus avoid going through town. I think I would feel trapped in this sort of environment, fighting through traffic just to get home. I wonder how Ninette copes with it after all the years she lived in the Prairies where a traffic jam was being second in line at the only traffic light in 30 miles. I suppose you adjust, but at what price?

Her garden is not what you would expect of the house or its occupants. An outsider might drive up to the house and take in the Doric columns guarding the front door, or I should say double-doors, and the Georgian façade and expect to see French windows leading to a classic, and perfectly manicured lawn fringed with the archetypical English herbaceous border. If they knew that my sister was from Scandinavian heritage by way of a Prairie upbringing they might have expected something more architectural and minimalist perhaps. In both cases they would be completely wrong. Ninette's favorite book as a child was The Lion, the Witch and the Wardrobe. She devoured the rest of the Narnia Chronicles with a voracity that bordered on addiction. Her garden reflects her childhood desire for a secret world to escape into, in fact multiple worlds connecting one to the other, each hidden by a secret passageway and offering its own adventure.

I decided to reacquaint myself with her garden and see what new treasures had been added since my last visit. My first step out of the French windows told me that my sister had been busy. The open flagged patio was still there, but was now covered with a network of large heavy, rustic, wooden beams inset with equally ancient-looking glass. "I see you found the new lean-to." I always love the way my sister refuses to use fashionable or inflated words when a basic description will do. I wondered what Stuart's law-firm associates thought of Ninette and her lean-to rather than arbor and her unorthodox garden. I could imagine them on their way home from a dinner party saying, "Stuart's wife's lovely but a little kooky don't you think?" I smiled and felt comfortable here, safe and at ease. My thoughts were broken by a voice calling me from the French Windows, "Would you like a cup of tea - or something stronger - it's almost Tiffin time." Tiffin was Stuart and Ninette's not so secret word for anything alcoholic. "Tea would be fine, thank-you," I replied and set off in search of mystery and wonder down the garden path.

As soon as I left the new lean-to I could hear running water, and as I followed the brick path and ducked low under the hanging branches of an apple tree I saw the source. Ninette had created a fountain using an old millstone as the centerpiece. Water was pumped up through the centre of the stone at just the right pressure to allow it to flow gently over the sides, down the stone and then over a pile of smooth beach pebbles on which the stone sat. A small wooden chair was positioned a few feet away under the bower of the apple tree. The spot was completely secluded and totally private. I sat for a few minutes and felt beautifully calm. I thought of Simon and how much he needed a spot such as this - if only he would use it. I decided I would come back to this spot as much as I could during my stay here.

As I continued my exploration I found a most delightful pond with flowering lilies, bulrushes and other grasses and reeds. Next to the pond, and reached by a small dock-like structure, was a small shed, although to call it a shed was to do it a disservice. It was not something you purchased from your local Home Depot or DIY centre. This hut had stained glass windows and other architectural features that had obviously come from many different, and ancient, sources. I went inside. I am not sure what I expected but it certainly wasn't what confronted me. The walls were covered with East Indian batiks depicting elephants, temples and mystical designs. A sofa bed took up the length of one wall and a bedside table featured an alarm clock, incense sticks and a holder. A thick Persian-looking rug completed the furnishings. The place looked lived in. Sitting on the sofa with the door open provided a perfect view of the pond. It was about as far away as you could get from typical English suburbia.

"Ah, there you are!"

I was broken out of my reverie by Ninette bearing a tray with tea, milk, lemon, homemade scones, thick clotted cream and raspberry jam. Perfect.

"So you've found my little hideaway."

"It's great Ninette, so different - but why."

"That's the question most of Stuart's colleagues ask, especially when they discover that we quite often sleep here instead of in the house."

"You sleep here?" I exclaimed.

"Surely you don't think I have succumbed completely to the life of a suburban upper middle-class housewife do you? This is the place we come to get away from our everyday life. It allows us to reconnect with each other and ourselves. In the summer it is like camping; we bring our sleeping bags down and fall asleep listening to the frogs. In winter we listen to the rain. We can escape to this different world anytime we want, when the stress of 'normal' life gets too much."

For a fleeting moment I wondered what else they got up to in this wonderfully romantic spot when the incense wasn't the only thing burning. I smiled to myself and thought 'go girl go'.

I thought back to my assessment of our two lives and reassessed whether I envied Ninette her lifestyle when compared to my freedom. I realized that she had found a way to, in part at least, have her cake and eat it. I did envy her, but the feeling would only last until I was crossing the Atlantic and looking down at my first sight of the Canadian coastline. It was really nice sitting here on the other side of Ninette's wardrobe, but it was still a temporary aberration in an otherwise well-ordered life.

"So, tell me, what are you working on at the moment?"

As we made short work of the scones, making sure that not one finger-licking morsel of cream escaped our attention, I told her the story of the QXCI and Simon, of Professor Nelson, Karen, Ryan and even Desirée, the real or imaginary character in the story.

"Tell me more about Simon."

It was an order not a request. My older sister was forever trying to see me married off and settled down. People are always like that. If they are married or living in a monogamous relationship they want everyone around them to be the same. If they are unhappy they seem to want to share the misery; if they are happy they are insufferably insistent that this wealth be shared. It seems to them the single life is somehow aberrant and that there must be something wrong with someone who would want to remain in that state.

"He's in his mid-fifties, married with two children - so he's too old and out of bounds, so you can forget about him being husband material."

"You sound as if you like him though."

"Yes, I do. He's a difficult boss, or I should say client, but there is something about him that fascinates me. He's definitely a challenge. On the one hand, he is really enthusiastic and lively and sure of himself. He has an incredibly positive attitude. And then there is this lost soul in search of a meaning to life. I also suspect that there is another Simon lurking just underneath the surface that few people see. I think this person is almost the complete opposite of the other and is totally subjugated."

"Is he religious?" Ninette was mopping up scone crumbs with a moist finger, chasing them around her plate.

"He wants to believe in something, anything, but has no idea what. I think he would like to have a faith, but finds it impossible to believe in anything that he doesn't have incontrovertible proof of. The QXCI has caused him a lot of problems because he feels it's too good to be true. I sometimes wonder if any amount of evidence will be enough to fully convince him that the device can indeed cure people."

"I find it curious," Ninette said, looking out at the pond which was now a hive of activity with dragonflies swooping and hovering and butterflies drinking from the hollyhocks that surrounded the far bank, "that some people can just believe, just like that and others can't. I once read an article that said that materialists believe that there is nothing at all but matter in motion, and naturalists believe that everything is made of lifeless, non-experiencing energy. And then there are the idealists, the believers I suppose, that say there is nothing but ideas, the mind or spirit."

I looked at my sister in a whole new light; I had never heard her speak like this before. I wondered whether her little hideaway with its eastern influence was having a meditative effect on her.

"I'd like to get to know him better, he isn't afraid to show his emotions, he makes me laugh and he really understands me. I feel good when I'm in his company." This was said abstractedly as I became lost in thought staring at two dragonflies mating on a lily pad. I immediately realized that I had said more than I intended, even more than I had admitted to myself.

"Ah, he makes you laugh and he understands you- there's a recipe for disaster if ever I saw one. I would have been less worried if you had said he was tall, dark and handsome. Men like that are common, but even with all his internal conflict he sounds like he's getting under your skin. He's married you say?"

"Yes, but I don't think it's much of a marriage, they never seem to do anything together. His wife is totally involved in her charity work and they seem to do their own thing most of the time. He travels a lot..." I trailed off.

"It's Okay dear, you don't have to convince me," she interrupted. And then that infuriating laugh that she had when I knew she was mocking me exploded from her, scattering pond life to the four corners of the garden. I felt the blood rush to my face and neck. I hadn't blushed in years and got up quickly and walked off the boardwalk and over to a long, narrow gravel area, which looked somewhat out of place in the well-managed clutter of this carefully planned garden. "What's this?" I asked, hoping she would not make something out of the quick change of topic.

"It's a boule court. You know - the French game of petanque. You have a small wooden ball called a cochonnet which you lob down the court, and then players take turns to lob heavy metal balls along the gravel to see who can get the closest. We can play later if you like."

"So it's like the Italian bocce ball then?"

"Very similar, except the balls are smaller, far heavier and made of metal. You throw them differently; you sort of flick them out the back of your hand. The French play it everywhere. If you drive through France you can see a boule playing area in the middle of most villages."

She picked up a small wooden ball and lobbed it to the far end of what I now knew was the boule court, and then from a small wooden box hidden under some bushes she brought out three cannon balls, or at least that's what they looked like. She lobbed one thirty or more feet toward the smaller ball, which was doing a great job of hiding itself in the gravel, and it came to rest an inch or so away. "Impressive," I said. "Let me try." I took one of the balls from her and tried to emulate her throwing style. The ball left my hand, travelled upwards rather than in the direction of the target and landed a few feet away from my toes. "It takes practice Hannah, we'll play some more over the next few weeks and make a boule player out of you yet."

As we walked back to the house Ninette grilled me about the work I was doing for Simon and asked whether I would be doing any research here in the U.K. I relaxed now that I was on safe ground. It felt good to talk to someone about the QX and my role in the writing of the book.

"My job is to gather information on the efficacy of this amazing device, to discover whether professional practitioners and patients believe that it works, and if it really does have the power to diagnose and treat almost any type of illness. I suppose I am trying to help Simon believe in the device by building a bridge between belief and disbelief. If I do my job well perhaps I can make the leap of faith small enough for Simon to attempt it. If that happens who knows what it might lead to?"

We walked in companionable silence for a while listening to the drone of bees and stopping along the way to admire flowers or just sit at some of the many spots that Ninette had found to position a swing, a log, a hammock, a stone bench or just a patch of soft grass.

" So, yes, I do have to do some work while I'm here Sis," I said.

"I thought you might."

"Simon has given me a few practitioners to contact, so I'll go and interview them, write up my notes and email them to him."

"So Leslie, how long have you being using the QXCI and how did you first hear about it?"

I am sitting in a small consulting room in a beautiful building in Henley-on-Thames, a beautiful town by the banks of the River Thames. It is the quintessential small English town, surrounded by lush woodlands that most people think of when they read a 1950s novel describing England. Henley is most famous for its annual rowing regatta held in July, where thousands of upper-class Brits spend the day drinking champagne, eating strawberries and cream, and of course mucking about on the water. The Royal Regatta was first held in 1839 and has grown over the years from a single afternoon event to one that now lasts five days. As many as 500 crews from around the world compete at the event while visitors party at one of Britain's premier social events. Henley is also well-known for its brewery and the quality of its foamy, nut-brown beverage that flows as fast and as consistently as the river.

Here in a quaint side street off the main drag, I am discussing the QXCI, which is anything but old and quaint. It almost seems out of place in this ancient setting. Leslie, in contrast to her surroundings, is a bright, smartly dressed woman in her mid-forties with a warm and open smile. Within seconds of my arrival she had put the kettle on for tea. The choice was extensive and included the standard Tetley tea bags along with a myriad of exciting herbal teas. I settled on a ginger green tea, which I knew would be both stimulating and also settling.

"About six years, shortly after I got stepped on and kicked in the head by a horse."

Well, that stopped me dead in my tracks and my jaw must have dropped because Leslie laughed out loud. She had a twinkle in her eyes and I knew we were going to get on just fine.

"Tell me more," I said.

"I was going through a lot of stress at the time - you know divorce, life changes all that crap. Anyway, one day I was out riding and my horse shied and I sort of slipped off, nothing serious, and I landed softly thinking, 'okay, that wasn't so bad'. Unfortunately, the horse became even more spooked and backed up, half stepping on my thigh and then, as he tried to avoid stepping on me again, he kicked me in the head. The result was that I suffered some memory problems, not full blown amnesia or anything but still disturbing. Where was I?"

Before I could answer she said, "Just joking."

I was really beginning to like Leslie. She had such a warm and open smile and her eyes had a cheeky, mischievous look so that I never knew when she was joking or being serious.

"Anyway, a friend recommended an alternative health practitioner that she had visited and I thought 'what the heck, I'll give him a try.' His name was James Revell and he worked out of an office just off Slough High Street. He told me all about this bio-feedback device he used and it somehow made sense to me, so I agreed to be hooked up to it. I didn't feel a whole lot better after my first visit although it was obvious the machine had provided him with a whole lot of information about me. He already knew about my encounter with the horse, so it wasn't as if I could have tested the device and seen if it came up with the diagnosis 'kicked in head by horse' or anything." She paused and reached for her tea.

"So, you went back and had some treatment?"

"Yes, I went back several times and Jim gave me some homeopathic preparations and over the next few weeks I began to feel a lot better. In fact, better than I had for a long time, mentally as well as physically."

"But how did all this lead to you becoming a practitioner yourself?" I asked.

She thought about this for a few seconds and then said, "It's a long story but I'll try to give you the condensed version. The company I was working for at the time was sold and I didn't feel like working for the new owners. Anyway, it was time for a change; everything else was changing in my life so I thought 'why not.' I went over to America to visit an old school chum, Jenny, who I had made contact with through the Friends Reunited Internet site. She was really into the alternative lifestyle so, while I was there, we took a spiritual psychology course. When I returned to England I went to Jim for a check-up. By this time the QX had become part of my life and it seemed natural to get a regular oil lube and filter, as Jenny had called it. When I told him about the course I had taken, and that I had a desire to set up in practice, he suggested that I take the training course he ran and become a QX practitioner. He felt that it might be difficult to sustain a practice as a spiritual psychologist alone, especially in a small town like Henley, but being able to offer QX sessions as well would make the whole thing viable."

"I see, and did it work that way? I mean is the practice viable?"

"Oh heavens yes, I see four clients a day, five days a week and I'm always booked two weeks ahead of time."

"I take it you are impressed with the device then," I said as I pointed to the little grey box that was now so familiar to me.

"It never ceases to amaze me, there is so much it can do - the results are truly amazing."

"That's some testimonial," I said.

"I'll go even further and say that it is an honor to work with a system such as this because it is based on caring and sharing. Dr. Nelson is a wonderful genius and so willing to share his knowledge for the greater good."

"Have you ever met him?" I asked.

She smiled and her eyes lit up her face in a nostalgic glow. "Yes, on several occasions. The one thing that comes across when you are with him is that his heart is in the system. The software program that interfaces with the device has his soul."

I made a few notes and the silence that surrounded us was comfortable. Leslie was happy talking about all this, happy to share, happy that she was helping more people learn about the device. If this were a religion, she would be a disciple. I thought about the QXCI and how Bill could so easily turn the power of the device and his own charisma into a cult with thousands of followers. He could be rich and supremely powerful overnight. I suppose the strength of the device, perhaps its true power, is in the freedom it allows users - the freedom to just do good.

"Do you advertise that you are a QXCI practitioner?" I asked.

"I have never needed to, word of mouth is all that is needed. The device is so good at what it does that people can't wait to talk about it."

I thought about the several calls that the voice-mail had picked up in the last thirty minutes or so and could well believe her.

"You say that people find out about it from friends - how do they react when you tell them that a machine and some computer software is going to interact with the energy in their body and tell them the status of their health?"

She smiled again. "The thing is that this is beyond the realm of what most people can understand; they can't even conceptualize this type of technology. I talk about the fact that we will be testing frequencies and using vibrations to diagnose and treat them. It is surprising how many people just accept it. It is as if people now accept the miraculous things technology can do and they no longer need to be able to understand them. I suppose it was much the same in our grandparents time when voices and music came out of a box that plugged into the wall." I nodded and smiled, encouraging her to continue. "The one program that people do sometimes have a problem understanding or accepting is the one that tests emotions. Some people believe that all emotion is stored in the brain but Candace Perch proved that the body stores the emotions in the form of peptides in different parts of the body."

"Really? I never knew that."

"Once you start working with the QX you learn so much. If I live to be a hundred I will only ever know a fraction of what the QX can do. That is probably the only sad thing about the device. It's potential is so much greater than anyone's ability to exploit it."

She looked sad, as if faced by an exciting challenge that was beyond her. I had seen the look before when interviewing Penny. These people could only ever scratch the surface - only help so many people. That is why everyone I have contacted has been so willing to talk to me and so happy to share their knowledge and experiences. If anything should convince Simon to believe in the QX, the combined belief of all the people that use or have been treated by the device should. That combined force is supremely powerful.

"What would you say to someone that has trouble believing that the QX really works?" I asked.

Once again Leslie smiled, this time beatifically like a nun to a disbeliever. You can't make people believe Hannah; they either do or they don't. They have to feel something in their inner being. The QX could cure someone, miraculously of some terrible disease and they might still think it just a coincidence. There is no way we can scientifically prove the QX works, at least not without many years of testing by top scientists, who almost certainly would have their own reasons for not wanting incontrovertible proof that the device is what it claims to be. People will believe or not. Those that I have treated know that the device has had a beneficial effect on them, even changed their lives. I would suggest, Hannah, that you tell your boss not to attempt to provide his readers with proof: it isn't important. What is important is that the device continues to treat people, and that word continues to spread, and as it does it will pick up speed until there is a critical mass of people that know, have faith if you like, in the ability of the

QX to change their life for the better. Oh dear, I think I rather sounded like an evangelical preacher there."

"You're not the first one, Leslie. Around three thousand practitioners are using the device and tens of thousands have been treated by it. Everyone I have talked to has a similar story about how the device and/or Bill made their life better. Tell me, why is the QX so special? I don't mean because it works, but why it works. Sorry, I'm probably not making myself clear."

She leaned forward enthusiastically, her arms stretched out and hands palm down, quietening me.

"No, I think I understand what you're asking. The device, or rather the device working in harmony with the software, is dealing with each individual separately, with no preconceived ideas about what it might or might not find. The practitioner, in this case me, has no influence on the device - it does its own thing. Dr. Nelson tells us that the name of the disease is not as important as what it behind it. It is the cause we need to identify so that we can stop its progress. We are not treating symptoms; we are identifying and treating the root cause."

"Did you have to take a lot of training and was it hard?" I asked.

"It was very tough, but so interesting and rewarding it wasn't like work. It was part long-distance learning and part practicum with

Jim. And I managed to go to one of Bill's conferences in Budapest, which was totally inspiring. It is there, with Bill and other practitioners, that you get to truly appreciate the magnitude of the device and the magnitude of Bill's genius. I think he is currently working on a more systematic training process, which is really needed as using the QX continually increases in complexity every time he updates and revises each program. Karen and Ryan Williams also offer excellent training programs and work closely with Bill on developing them."

"So you don't need to be a doctor then to be able to set up practice and treat people with the device?"

I could see that I had hit a nerve and decided to wait in silence and allow her to compose her thoughts; after all, I am not an investigative journalist.

"The thing is, I don't diagnose anything, the QX does. And even then it doesn't come right out and say for instance, that somebody has cancer. It will say that the energy that represents cancer may be indicated and therefore I advise the client to go and see their medical practitioner. The device treats other illnesses in the same way as an acupuncturist would via the acupuncture meridians. It will also balance chakras and assist with emotional disturbances."

I sensed there was more, so I sat and waited.

"The bottom line is that I don't think of myself as curing people. Anybody treating disease is in a precarious position, so using the device, I help people reduce the stress in their lives and in their bodies. I alert them to the issues they face and what they should do to get their bodies back onto a healthy track. Officially we are not allowed to diagnose. Perhaps one day when the authorities really understand the power of this device they will stop trying to prevent people being helped. So many lives could be saved."

"So, can you tell me about any success stories you have had?"

"Well there have been many, but once again I have to be careful how I explain this to you. One of my very first experiences with the QX was with a fourteen-year old girl who came to me after she had lost her eyebrows and eyelashes and was now losing her hair. She had been diagnosed as having chronic fatigue syndrome, but her doctors weren't coming up with any bright ideas about how to treat her. Her mother brought her to see me and I hooked her up to the QX. I ran the standard tests on her and it showed she was extremely low in B vitamins and that her digestive system was out of balance. I suggested she take some vitamins and amino acids, among other things. I then taught her some stress management techniques and ways to focus and centre herself. The following month I saw her again and carried on with much the same treatment. When her Mum called to make the third appointment she was crying; she said she couldn't believe the difference in her daughter. I still see the girl riding her bike to school. All her hair has grown back and she is completely back to normal."

"That's a neat story Leslie. It's so good to hear how a life can be turned around. So simple too, no incredible miracle, just sound common sense once you knew what you were dealing with. That's what impresses me most about the QX, it really is a tool to help practitioners see the truth behind an illness."

"Absolutely Hannah, I wouldn't want people to think that this was some miracle machine that can cure anybody of anything one hundred percent of the time. Life just isn't like that. We are still in control of our own bodies and have to be willing to do what the device and the practitioner recommends. Most of the time it's about correcting imbalances in the body. The bottom line is often really simple. The complexity of it is discovering what the bottom line is and that is the genius of the QX."

I was dying to hear another success story and hoped Leslie would not need to wrap up the interview quite yet. I was not disappointed, as a few seconds later she launched into another story.

"I had another woman who was due to have a thyroid operation and came to see if I could do anything while she waited her turn to get the operation on the National Health Service. The QX showed immediately that she had an extreme amount of stress in the thyroid so I used a series of homeopathics recommended by the QX to cleanse and stimulate it. When she first came to me she had a lump the size of a 10 pence coin, but after a month it was down to the size of a pea. She carried on with the homeopathics and never needed the surgery. I just love it when I can prevent the need for the surgeon's knife. I really hate invasive procedures unless they are a last option."

"Have you treated cancer patients?" I asked, holding my breath, as I knew this was a difficult subject.

"Hmm, I have put it out to the Universe that I would be willing to work with cancer patients. It would be imprudent of me to say that the QX can detect cancer, but I can say that there is stress on a particular organ and that they should get it checked out by their doctor. If they have already been diagnosed with Cancer I advise them to carry on with their traditional treatment and then treat them myself with vibrational frequencies and homeopaths. I have several patients in this category, mostly friends or friends of friends. I have one friend who had radiation treatment for skin cancer, which left his face quite badly burned. The cancer started to come back and he couldn't get in to see the specialist for several weeks. In the meantime, I treated him using the special program offered by the QX. As it happens he was extremely sensitive to the vibrations generated by the program and could tell exactly what part of the body the device was treating. As you know Hannah, the vibrations would have been occurring in the relevant acupuncture meridians, not on the site of the skin cancer itself." I nodded, although in truth I had forgotten, and imagined somehow the device treating the actual localized spot itself. Silly me.

"Unfortunately he was away a lot on business and our schedules clashed so much I couldn't continue the therapy as much as I would have liked. It worried me a lot that I couldn't do more so I decided to try something I hadn't done before, and that was to put the frequencies in a water and alcohol base, which he took internally. The results were good and the spot on his face has disappeared. I'm not sure if it's gone completely, but I am sure we helped it to regress."

"Frequencies in water curing someone? That's a bit hard to believe Leslie."

"I agree Hannah, for many people it is. I am even experimenting with virtual testing where the person isn't close by at all. This blows the mind of many people and I rarely mention it as it really pushes people's belief system to their outer limits."

I thought to myself that this was one story I would definitely not pass on to Simon. It would ruin all the good work I have done so far in convincing him that this device is for real.

"Okay, why should I believe in virtual testing? I have no trouble believing in the power of the device when it is measuring the vibrational frequencies running through someone's body. I can totally accept that you can then send back into the body other electrical or vibrational frequencies to correct faulty ones. But doing it without the patient being in the room - that's far fetched."

Leslie smiled. "Do you have a mobile on you?" I must have looked puzzled because she quickly said, "Cell phone, sorry. We both speak English but there's still a language gap!" I nodded and rummaged around in my purse before bringing out a stylish bright red piece of technology that had really impressed me in the store.

"I rented it for my stay in England from Virgin," I said.

"Could you call Simon for me and ask him a question?" I nodded and started to dial the number. She reached across and laid her hand on the phone and said, "No need to actually do it, but you could couldn't you?"

"Well of course I could." I replied.

"And you could speak to him even though he is several thousand miles away with no lines between you - the vibrations of your voice would reach him?"

I was beginning to see where she was leading with this and thought I would cut her off at the pass. "But that's different, I have a piece of technology and so does he. He receives my signal."

She leaned forward, as people do when they are trying to convince you of something. "But it is the same, don't you see? You create a frequency here in England that is sent to him, which he then receives through his phone's aerial but, and this is the big one - those frequencies are not only received by his phone, they also flow through millions of other people as they journey from your phone to his. So why should it be so hard for people to believe that positive therapeutic vibrations can be sent in the same way. I know it's hard to believe, and I am only just getting my head round it myself, but I have tried it a few times with startling results. It's one of my experiments."

This was a subject that was too big for me to go into at this stage, but I thought it would make a good follow up to Simon's book if he felt inclined to go out on a limb and write a sequel. I decided that I was close to overstaying my welcome, so chose my next question carefully to allow for a wider scope to Leslie's answer.

"Tell me about your favorite QX program."

She only had to think for a few seconds before answering. "Ah, that would be NLP, Neuro-Linguistic Programming. This detects trauma within the body, whether it's spiritual, emotional or physical. I had a teenage girl who was experiencing chronic back problems. She had tried many different forms of treatment including visiting physiotherapists and chiropractors, but no one seemed to be able to help her. The NLP program picked up a trauma at age four. Her mother remembered that she had fallen off a slide onto her back at that age. She had forgotten the trauma but her body had not. The QX allows the body to clear these traumas, thus relieving the physical symptoms."

I sat back and waited, hoping that she would provide another example. Interviewing a highly respectable, intelligent and erudite professional with excellent, non-sensational true case studies was gold dust: Simon would be over the moon.

Leslie didn't disappoint me. "I also had a middle aged man who had suffered for years with digestive problems. When I ran the NLP test program on him the years 11 and 25 came up as important. He was quite amazed and said he was brought up on a farm and at age eleven he had been kicked in the stomach by a cow. At age 25 he had been in a car crash, been thrown clear and the car had rolled over him. He ended up having surgery on his stomach and pancreas."

"So the physical problems may have been cured, but the body is holding on to the symptoms, or a shadow of the symptoms due to the mental trauma." I said.

"Yes, something like that." I could see that she was getting tired. We had been talking for almost two hours and, although she had assured me that she had allowed plenty of time for the interview, I was beginning to feel that I had taken up too much of her day.

"Well, thank you so much for all that you have told me. Your work is fascinating and you have added to the many stories I have collected over the last few months. Is there anything else you feel I should pass on to Simon?"

"I've enjoyed meeting you Hannah and talking about my work. I suppose the thing I want to finish on is that the QXCI prioritizes the primary concerns, the things that are most out of balance with the patient. It chooses what is important, not the patient or me. My job is to hang in there and work with the device to peel away the layers of the onion and discover the real problem, the root cause. A patient may arrive complaining of tennis elbow, but the QX may recognize that their heart is under extreme pressure. I then need to treat the heart, even though the patient is more concerned with his or her elbow. The QX really excels at being able to detect trauma frequencies. The device will often point out a specific spot and indicate stress there, even when the patient is not suffering any pain in that area. When questioned, the patient will tell you about an old injury. This happened to me a short while ago when the QX indicated a muscle at the back of a gentleman's knee. I asked him if he had been hit there; he laughed and told me that he had been shot in the back of the leg. I am sure, Hannah, that if you ask for these sort of stories from practitioners and patients you will come up with dozens of them. Whenever I meet with other QXCI practitioners at Quantum Life or Maitreya Institute seminars or conferences we share these sorts of stories, and still get a buzz at how totally accurate the device is."

I thanked Leslie for her time and the enormous amount of information she had shared with me. We shook hands and she asked me to keep in touch and perhaps next time I was over for a visit we could meet for lunch. I said that I'd like that and promised to email her on my return to Canada.

I went back to where I had parked Ninette's car, a sporty little red Renault convertible. She had lent me the car for the day and had driven Stuart to the railway station in the Range Rover, so there was no need to rush back. The Renault was fun to drive and using my trusty AA road atlas I decided to see a little more of the Thames Valley countryside. As I looked at the map names such as Pishill, Play Hatch, Hare Hatch, Lower Assendon and Cockpole Green all caught my attention. The British have such great names for their villages and each one has a completely logical meaning connected with past times and past customs, although Cockpole Green made me shake my head. I decided to head north-east and head for Marlow, which I had heard was a smaller, but no less picturesque, version of Henley-on-Thames.

I thought a walk by the Thames, a pub lunch and later a stop for afternoon tea might be a very British thing to do.

As I drove I started to recap in my mind the dozens of interviews I had carried out for Simon. Some I had visited, but many had been by telephone; the one thing they all had in common was that they all believed in the QXCI. Patients and practitioners alike had provided a tremendous amount of anecdotal evidence that something very special was happening once the handshake between the device and the patient took place.

I remember Simon telling me about the mass of anecdotal evidence amassed on reincarnation. I thought it strange at first because he was making a case for believing in something without having irrefutable scientific evidence, but he was just playing devil's advocate. He said that if you were sitting on a bench and someone came round the corner and said there was a herd of elephants stampeding toward you, you might not believe them. But if several people, one after the other, said the same thing, you would probably start to believe them and get out of the way. Well, I have more than a few people telling me the same story and I'm pretty sure its not mass hysteria, especially as my case studies are spread far and wide around the world.

I passed through Mill End but didn't see any mill. A signpost on the corner of a small road to my left announced Hambleden, Rockwell End and Skirmett but I resisted the temptation.

The biggest issue that prevents the QXCI from being used more extensively is the fact that in many countries it is illegal to use it for diagnosis or treatment. Practitioners are often in a very difficult situation and even though the device may detect strong frequencies of cancer in a patient they cannot say that the patient actually has cancer. All they can do is to let the patient know that they have detected stress in a particular organ and advise them to see their doctor.

Ben Bailey, a practitioner from Florida, had talked to me about how the QXCI weaves together so many different modalities. He mentioned dozens, but the ones I could recall without the aid of my notes were iridology, macrobiotics, reflexology, auras, chakras and acupuncture. The device and the software are so complex that Simon and I will never be able to do more than scratch the surface of its capabilities. I began to wonder if there was anyone, other than Professor Nelson of course, who understood or could use all of the QXCI's programs and potential. I doubt it very much. It was Ben, I remember, who described the initial 'handshake' as a three minute test that establishes a quick positive first impression. He said it was electrophysiological and that 7,000 items are tested. This means the computer is making a couple of million mathematical computations in the space of a few minutes. What sort of mind could have developed the software that made this possible? I remember Simon telling me that Professor Nelson was a self-taught computer programmer, making it even more staggering that he could create this program.

A sign informed me that Medmenham was just a mile away. I thought I might stop and check it out.

Some of the more experienced QXCI users, especially those that taught new practitioners, had given me their own unique insight into why the device was so successful. One such man, Gerry, had said that nature is fractal and that there is no such thing as '1+1=2'. Change is constant and the QXCI adapts to that change process. When a patient is hooked up to the computer via the device, they become one with the device; the patient follows the device and the device follows the patient. They are in tandem. Therapy is carried out in fractions and milliseconds and the device is able to adapt to wherever the patients wants or needs to go. The whole process is non-invasive; there are no urine or blood samples taken, just energy readings. The system looks at the patient concisely, clearly and objectively. The practitioner is only the guide. He went on to say that the device provides an unbelievably accurate look at the patient's subconscious report on the cause of the disease.

Medmenham is very small and I stop for just a few minutes and look at the local church. I discover that the name is derived from the old English words 'medeme' + 'ham', which means moderately-sized homestead. As I said earlier, there is a sort of logic to these English names, although exactly why someone would call their village this, I have no idea. Perhaps somewhere there are village names that mean small hay cart or irregular shaped duck pond and the like.

I'm back on the road. Driving these small roads in the middle of the day with the sun shining on me is extremely cathartic. It's allowing me to clear my head and consider some of the key issues raised over the last few months.

Penny told me something that I found really interesting. She had a patient that had been diagnosed with cancer and the QXCI didn't pick it up. She called Bill to ask why this would happen when the device was usually so accurate. He told her that if her patient wasn't reacting to the cancer, it might be the reason she got it in the first place; her body was not recognizing it as foreign and therefore wasn't trying to get rid of it. I remembered Leslie saying that the device can only show someone's response to a disease, which made sense given the way the device works.

So if the QXCI is not really allowed to diagnose or treat people, what is its role? A practitioner in France, Marie explained to me that the device stops people from being blind and helps them see the direction they need to go, to help them become healthy and stay that way. She told me that it gave people the opportunity to tune their three natures: body, mind and spirit. She said that this was the greatest gift a person on earth can have.

All of a sudden I realize that I have been driving on auto-pilot. I have been oblivious to the last few miles and am now in Marlow High Street which is full of small quaint shops, lots of brickwork, colour and people. All of a sudden I feel ravenous and decide to find a typical quaint English pub. I have always found that pub fare in England is good, especially if one avoids city centers and modern establishments. I decide to get off the main drag and look for something small and old. At the end of the high street, I turn left onto West Street in search of the perfect place to lunch. And there it is just down the road: The Ship, a white stucco building that certainly looks old enough and quaint enough to fit the bill.

As I go in I have to duck through the low door - people of yore were definitely small! I sit down at a table and a few minutes go by before I remember where I am and go to the bar to order a drink. I point to one of the beers on tap and ask for a glass. "A half-pint then love," the barman asks. "Yes please," and I remember that people in England drink half-pints and pints, not glasses. I glance around at the regulars and a few of them smile back. I ask for a lunch menu and get quite an elaborately bound affair. I take it back to my table and spend a wonderful fifteen minutes reading about all the local delights I could indulge in. In the end I decide on a ploughman's lunch.

While I am waiting for my food I wander up to get another drink and ask the barman how old the pub is and whether the beams, which are massive pieces of ancient looking timber, are original. He tells me that the pub is sixteenth-century and the beams came from ships of that time. I wonder how? Perhaps they were salvaged from shipwrecks and had been involved in sea battles with pirates. Whatever, they are not giving up their secrets. My food has arrived. They must have hungry ploughman out this way because in front of me is about a pound of cheese, a hunk of rustic bread that could feed a prisoner for a week, half a dozen cherry tomatoes, cucumber, little white pickled onions, and some brown chunky stuff that smells like pickle, oh ... and a piece of celery. When I move the bread I also discover three thick slices of ham, obviously cut from a full ham and not shaved thin like we get from the grocery store deli's back home.

An hour and a half later and 'pogged,' a word meaning full up, which I just learned from another tourist visiting from Yorkshire, I am back out on the street. After talking to a couple of locals I decide to walk down to see Marlow's pride and joy - an iron bridge. Why the interest in a bridge? Because of a coincidence I discovered when talking to my Buckinghamshire buddies in the pub. The bridge was built by William Tierney Clarke, who also designed a very similar bridge, the Chain Bridge that links Buda and Pest. I really enjoy synergistic experiences such as this. Here I decide, on the off-chance, to visit this town while researching a book for Simon, which had its genesis in Hungary, and stumble on a bridge that has a sister in Budapest.

Anyway, as I turn the corner, I am impressed with the bridge in all its iron glory, painted white and stretching across the River Thames rather majestically. I wonder if Simon crossed the Chain Bridge spanning the Danube. I know it's silly but I feel very close to him at this moment.

In the middle of the bridge I stop and look back at All Saints Church and its 170-foot spire. It's an impressive sight, especially here in the middle of the bridge with the Thames stretching out in either direction, peppered with motor cruisers, rowers and even a tiny ancient river steamer looking very bucolic, but polluting the atmosphere somewhat.

I wander down to the lock the locals had also said was a must-visit. Locks are fascinating things; they are water elevators for boats, managed by lock keepers who always seem to be interesting and often eccentric characters. Locks are a hive of activity, and bustle with people jumping off boats to grab an ice cream or a soda before getting on with their journey, either higher or lower than they were before. I can see the church from here and when the hubbub ceases for a second, I can hear the weir with water thundering from one level to the next as the river drops to its new level.

I look at the people around me: fat and thin, tall and short, old and young, happy and sad, black and white and every shade in between. They all have health issues, everyone of them - it's part of being alive. Many will be seeing specialists, some for their heart, others for their kidneys or liver or any other part of their body. Some will have a disease and not even know it. Some will be predisposed to disease and harboring time-bomb genes waiting to go off who knows when. If only they could all be tested by the QXCI; they would be so much more aware of what is happening within their bodies. What might happen and what past events are still affecting them? But their modern-day healthcare is piecemeal. Doctors treat their symptoms as and when they appear, calling in specialists that concentrate on one element of the body, as if it worked in isolation from the rest of the organism.

The QXCI is holistic; that's the key! It treats the patient as a whole, it has no preferences as to what it checks or doesn't check. It has no preconceptions. It looks at the whole person and discovers imbalances and corrects them. Simple really.

I wish Simon were here. I wish I could share this with him. I miss him. That's probably the first time I have really admitted that to myself. I need someone that understands me, who makes me laugh, that really gets me. I wonder if he needs me? He called me his metaphysical guide once. I wonder what he is doing now?

"There you are! How was your day out Hannah?"

I am sitting by the mill stone fountain and have been for the last hour. When I came home the Range Rover was not parked outside and I suspected that Ninette was picking Stuart up from the railway station. My work for Simon is almost done. I have to pull my notes together from this trip and write them up, but that's about it. We may do a debriefing at some stage, but I had better start thinking about what to do next - except I don't want there to be a next. I want this to continue, it feels good and it feels right.

I realize Ninette is standing over me.

"Wake up Hannah, you look miles away."

"Sorry Ninette, I was. What did you say?"

"I asked how your day went. Did the interview go well? Did you get what you wanted?"

I gave her a condensed version of the day's events but left out my ruminations about Simon. Digby and Jasper came tearing up to us with Stuart a few seconds behind them. Sometimes he's like a big kid, chasing the dogs around and wrestling with them on the grass. I smile, he is a nice guy.

"Hey Sis, I read some of that material you gave me on this QX thing, it's really interesting. Does it really work?"

"As far as I can gather from my interviews with patients and practitioners, it seems to work exceptionally well, yes."

"Ah, but tell me, what you really think of it? At the end of the day what's your take?"

Unlike most lawyers I have met, Stuart sets great store on what people he trusts think about things. All day he works with facts, often manipulating them to suit his needs, but nevertheless using facts, not opinions. But in this case, outside of a court of law, he was in search of a professional opinion. I chose my words carefully.

"Stuart, I think the device is 20 years ahead of its time. There is no other machine like it in the world; it is a totally amazing interface of computer technology with the human body, the human mind and the human spirit - it is the future of healthcare."

"Wow, the only problem now Sis, is how do you sell that to the rest of the world? Especially the millions of people and businesses with a vested interest in the traditional methods of dispensing medical treatment?"

The question hung on the air. I needed someone to hug - and he was an ocean away.

THE PROMISE FULFILLED

I t is four in the morning and the words are coming, but slowly. It feels as if each one demands all of my attention, all of my energy. Even when they appear they don't look completely formed, as if the journey to the page has somehow corrupted them slightly. I learn to love them though, warts and all - after all, it's not what they are but what they can become that counts. Later, like a plastic surgeon, I will perform surgery on them, a nip and tuck, a lift and separate until they are as beautiful as they were in my mind's eye.

The book that was to be the simple telling of the story of the miraculous QXCI is twelve months overdue. Deadlines have come and gone along with the seasons, and now it feels like winter, a time of hibernation and hunkering down, just when I need the revitalization of spring. In reality it is late May and my office is still hot from the day's heat and sixteen hours of computer-generated warmth.

My mind is overtaxed with all that I have learned on this journey. The industry of health and the science of quantum biology, my own faith and the importance of our metaphysical being fight with each other for dominance. I am still struggling with the leap of faith I have made in accepting that a little grey box and some computer software can read and assess the energy radiating through our bodies to such a fine degree that it can even recognize trauma that occurred during the nine months prior to our birth.

But then again, I had difficulty believing at first that our traditional healthcare system, especially that portion controlled by the pharmaceutical companies, could be so frighteningly corrupt and self-serving. And to discover that our doctors, those self-appointed deities who seem to be held in such high regard by 'Joe Public', are easy, sometimes willing, victims of corporate hype is just as unbelievable. We seem to almost hypnotically suspend our belief in human frailties where doctors are concerned, and increasingly or so it seems, the more arrogant they become.

My biggest question has been 'how can the QXCI be so far ahead of the rest?' We always say 'if it seems too good to be true then it must be'. But if we analyze this statement we can see how ridiculous it is. Based on this, we would dismiss anything or everything without addressing any factual, statistical or scientific data. An eighteen-month-old Ontario child wandered out of a house in the early hours of the morning in minus 20-degree temperatures a few months ago and was found several hours later face down in the snow. Her little heart had stopped beating for more than two hours by the time she was discovered and paramedics managed to reach her. They miraculously managed to get her breathing again but still feared for her life; she was certainly going to lose fingers and toes, if not arms and legs to frostbite and possibly gangrene. One month later she left hospital alive, happy and all in one piece. Sound too good to be true? Certainly. Is it a well-documented fact? Absolutely!

All this is swirling around in my mind as I try to piece together the elements of the QXCI story, which has become inextricably linked with my own search for understanding about who and what I am, and ultimately my faith, or lack of it.

Many months ago I started out planning to write a biography and have ended up writing about something that only a few superior minds can truly understand. In truth, I have barely scratched the surface of this intrigue. I feel as if my metaphysical struggle has manifested itself, not in some new attempt at spiritual rebirth, but in accepting and embracing a scientific philosophy that matches any religion in its power to affect the lives of those it touches.

It is now five o'clock in the morning and the sky is brightening as I realize that I am back where I started all those years ago - in England, sitting in an ancient church in Beverley, North Yorkshire waiting for a sign from God, except that now I have made a leap of faith, of sorts. I believe in the QXCI, but is that belief incontrovertible? I suspect doubts lingering on the fringes of my psyche, and realize that I am still waiting for a sign that may never come.

Mood swings account for much of my inability to take the progress of evidence through to belief and build on it from one day to the next. Like most things in my world of changing moments, clarity is a transitory guest, but one that rarely outstays its welcome.

I stand up and press the key that sends my computer to sleep. I've struggled enough for one day, fought enough demons. Another five hundred words have found their way onto my shimmering page. Do they exist in the real world, or are they just so many electronic impulses created by me and kept prisoner by a glorified abacus until I free them?

In the bathroom, I look at myself in the mirror and a tired old man looks back. Inside this shell, a mere fabrication of who I really am, there is hidden a young and vibrant version screaming to be let out. How can I begin to bring faith into my life or accept the true wonder of Bill's creation, when I can't acknowledge who or what I have become?

The final stages of writing the book have arrived, most of the pieces are in place and the players have told their stories. My job now is to tie it all up into a neat bundle with no loose ends. But blank pages still haunt me. When will I know it is finished? Will there be a sign? Why can't I just believe?

I continue to stare at my reflection and see waning hope; I'm a few small steps away from despair. I think about what it would be like to end it all, to just be finished with it, this great effort. Not just the book but everything: life and the struggle it brings me every day. I wish I didn't feel this way but I do. Life seems to be so much disillusionment, punctuated by short snaps of happiness and even shorter periods of peace. Sometimes I just long for peace, a time away from being me, being what people expect me to be, putting on a brave face. I don't like the person that is me, the character I have become to hide myself from myself. Every now and then I catch a glimpse of myself from a distance, as if watching from afar, and I don't like what I see. What hope is there for someone who doesn't like himself? I often find myself excruciating, and shudder as if it is someone else embarrassing himself. I have become good at hiding behind humour like so many well-known comedians that have committed suicide. People can't understand why such happy people have such sad secret lives. I have always felt somewhat of a kindred spirit with the legion of comedians who have taken their own lives. Why do I liken myself to those that have gone before me? Am I really thinking of suicide as a way out, a way forward, an escape or just another angle? Perhaps I am just craving attention. A little shit thinking only of himself and not the people in his life that care. What would they do, what would they think, how long would they grieve before picking up the pieces to start again?

I think of all the times I have been driving and considered just not turning the wheel - smashing into the truck in front, or slamming into a hydro pole or just launching into space and falling spectacularly into a ravine in a ball of fire.

And then, as I always do when I'm down, I snap out of it, pull my face up out of the dirt and self pity, and tell myself: "Simon, you need to get away - and fast."

The decision to go to Tofino was an obvious one and it came to me in that never-never land between wakefulness and sleep when body and mind battle each other for control. Evelyn Waugh, in one of his books, had a character, a very old man, who was frightened to go to sleep in case he failed to wake up in the morning. He used to stay up all night drinking, alcohol eventually settling the battle between body and mind. I know what he meant: I have always had a fear of waking up dead. Life is full of paradox.

Of course, this once again related back to a lack of spirituality in my life. I needed an escape and time to reflect on how much the book and the device had really taken over my life.

As I drive to Tofino, I start to think about the personal journey of growth I have taken since meeting Karen and Ryan in that coffee shop in Victoria. From being well within my comfort zone and writing their business plan, I travelled to Budapest and a strange world where reality dissolved into unexplainable relationships with characters like the mystical Desirée and the very real Professor Nelson. And then I met the QXCI with all its mysterious power for good, restricted by the corporate power and greed of pill-and-potion pushers, modern day alchemists. And finally, I discovered almost unbelievable tales of people being healed by a device small enough to hold in the palm of your hand - stories of hope and salvation and rebirth.

This is the last leg of that journey and I am still not sure what I will discover when I get there. The end of the road? Inevitably. But there are so many more ends to consider: the book finished at last, belief in the QXCI - without reservation, belief in and acceptance of myself; and my search for faith, but in what?

Was I always fully in command? Or did I lose control occasionally? Karen and Ryan, Bill and Desirée, and Hannah had such an enormous effect on my psyche that they have undoubtedly changed who I am. The question is: for better or for worse? And when everything settles down and personalities recede into the past, will I like myself more or less than when I started? Will I understand myself better, or will I be left with more questions than answers?

Karen and Ryan taught me to take myself less seriously, to open up, to care for my physical being and to recognize that there is a spiritual element that resides within me. For the longest time I was unsure of what part they were going to play in my life, especially life after the book. I am still unsure. They unsettle me in so many ways because they are so different from me. I am the ultimate entrepreneur, self-focused and a workalcoholic with little time to consider anything outside of my immediate business activities. They too are entrepreneurs, but inhabit a different world than mine. Their world is tied closely to the earth, with faith and a deep-rooted concern for humanity. But for all that, they are true entrepreneurs, far more natural than me. They believe we are all here for a purpose and seem to have a clear idea of theirs.

A few weeks ago Karen gave birth to a boy and they named him Sean Mission because they believe he has a mission here on earth. I suppose the more I am around this fascinating and wonderful couple the more I start to question my position of total agnosticism. It is hard for me to accept, but I think they are right and that we all have a mission; I just wish I knew what mine was.

I pass through Nanaimo (a town of 75,000 souls) surrounded by incredible natural beauty. It is home to an odd event called the 'Bathtub Race' where people create seaworthy vessels from old bathtubs and race around a gruelling 36 mile course. An old mining town when coal was gold, Nanaimo now has a dying city centre from which an expanding strip mall radiates, speeding along the highway like ivy. It's as if new construction at the tip of the organism is trying to outpace the decay at its roots. Still, in spite of 'big box' stores and other retail giants, it seems to hang onto some of its past charm. The power of ancient trees, majestic mountains and the cobalt ocean balance the scales, but in a battle they can never win, not in the short-term at least.

Hannah, wonderful Hannah, allowed me to see and understand that the spiritual building blocks that continually confront me were there for a reason. And that the metaphysical expedition I was on would result in a new and stunning view of the world from a peak that was just one of many I would reach during my life. Hannah is so much younger than me in years but, if I allow myself the luxury of believing in reincarnation, albeit fleetingly, I can see that she has been here many more times than I. She has a worldly wisdom that comes from a depth of experience that couldn't possibly have come from just one lifetime, especially such a short one.

One of the reasons I have started to think that reincarnation is a real possibility, is that from time to time I meet people who have an impact on me that is so much stronger than can be explained by personality or even pheromones. I feel that I have known them before and we have shared experiences. The intensity of this feeling can be overwhelming and sometimes frightening. The strangest of these meetings occur when the feelings are reciprocated and the other person feels drawn to me by some inextricable link. If this only happened with females that I am attracted to and feel drawn to, I could explain it away by sexual attraction. But that is not the case. Occasionally, the reverse happens and the hairs on the back of my neck stand up when I meet someone. They are, outwardly at least, perfectly normal pleasant people. And, I hate them - sometimes they scare me and I have this intense feeling that they have done me or my loved ones some harm in the past. The fact that I have never met them before in my life does not persuade my body chemistry to allow my hackles to lower. This has even occurred with people that on a surface level I actually like, could even be friends with, but somewhere our paths have crossed and a battle has been fought. If not in this world, then where? The effect when you meet someone who affects you like this is startling. I am sure there are other explanations as to why these people make us feel like they do, but the only explanation that I am comfortable with is that we have experienced life together before, and our lives have become inextricably linked. The question is why? Do they come back into our lives, and us into theirs, with a warning or some advice perhaps, or just to nudge us in a certain direction? Are the feelings real or just memories? The big question is that if I believe that we have shared experiences outside of this life, why have I not taken the leap of faith and become a card-carrying member of the reincarnationist party? Because of doubt and Descartes, the guy that said "I think therefore I am." Recently I had a discussion with Hannah about Descartes and his theories on doubt - I think she got frustrated with me - but he believed that the only thing one couldn't doubt was ones existence. Beyond that, there is always doubt. How much evidence does one need? Is there ever enough? It depends on who you are I suppose.

Many years ago when I was living in England, I saw a television documentary, made by a well-respected investigative reporting team, which dealt with the issue of reincarnation. The team was well known for exposing shams, whether by conmen, companies or politicians. In this particular show they looked at several ordinary people claiming that they were reincarnated. I don't remember many of the stories, but one has stuck with me over the years and probably is the cornerstone of my shaky foundation for leaning toward a belief that we travel this earth more than once.

The TV journalists had scoured the world's media looking for stories that might lead them to some sort of truth. They had stumbled on a story in an Indian newspaper about a strange boy in a village outside of Delhi who was demanding to go and see his wife and children. As the child was only nine years old he was thought to be mentally disturbed, but the newspaper for some reason had followed up on the story and interviewed both the boy and his parents, who were peasant farmers. The boy appeared sane in every other way and there was no sign of any mental illness. The only explanation therefore was that the boy was in touch with the spirit world and therefore blessed. He became the centre of attraction in the region but continued to be only interested in reuniting with his family.

Enter the British documentary team who visited the boy's village, interviewed his parents for the show and talked extensively with the boy himself. He was an intelligent child with an unruly mop of thick black hair and a confidence that seemed out of place for a peasant boy dealing with Western journalists. They discovered that the boy's story held up to scrutiny. He was not only consistent in his answers, but that when probed, his knowledge of his 'other' family was extensive. He claimed that he was married and had a wife and two children, and that they had something to do with televisions and radios, items that were not to be found in his village.

The team started to investigate the child's story, and putting several clues together, decided to call electrical stores in several key cities across India. Eventually they found a store in the suburbs of Calcutta that was run by a widowed woman with the name the child had told them was his wife's. She also had two children with the same names the boy had mentioned. They persuaded the boy's parents to allow them to take him to Calcutta and see if he could recognize the woman. In Calcutta, as the team, with cameras rolling, turned down a back street, the boy pointed excitedly toward an electrical shop. As soon as the van came to a stop the boy jumped out of the vehicle and into the store with the cameraman in hot pursuit. The woman behind the counter looked as if she was about to throw the urchin out until he piped up, "Shana, why did you move the counter to the front of the shop?" The journalists, who by this time had caught up with the cameraman, asked the woman if she had moved the counter. She replied that she had, but that had been more than ten years ago and how did this child know her name? She looked frightened. The child again asked 'why?'

but this time more forcefully. The woman ignored the child and talked directly to the journalists. "Who are you? What do you want with me?" The on-screen presenter told her who they were and what they were doing and gave her 4000 rupees for her trouble. The boy chimed in, "How have you been, my wife?" The earlier fear, dissipated by the westerner's money, returned to her face and the presenter quickly asked her to answer the boy's earlier question. She told them that her husband had been robbed and murdered a little over ten years ago and as she was often alone in the shop she could watch the rest of the store better when she stood at the till at the front. With a little more prompting she told them that times had been hard since her husband had died. He hadn't believed in banks and had died without telling her the secret location of their savings, which he had buried somewhere. All this time, her eyes never left the little boy.

While all this was happening the boy had been half watching some children kicking a ball around on some wasteland opposite the store. The cameraman panned to the boy who pointed and quietly said the names of the children he claimed were his. The presenter asked the woman if her children were playing outside and she nodded. "Can you go and bring your children here?" the presenter asked the boy. He nodded and walked across the street. Two minutes later the family was reunited. The television show only gave snippets of what went on between the boy and the woman, but enough to show the viewer that the child knew things about the family that he couldn't or shouldn't have known. The woman was loath to believe the story and accept that the child was her husband returned in a different body. What convinced her was having her life-savings returned to her. The boy did indeed know where the money was hidden.

At this point in the story I was still not completely convinced. It all seemed too pat. After all, the child could have been psychic, a mind reader, or it could all have been some sort of scam with the investigative team being conned for a change.

But the team was well-known for seeking out every angle of a story and decided to go one step further in their search for truth. They got autopsy photographs of the dead husband from the police showing the wound - he had been shot in the head at close range. After talking to several experts on the subject of reincarnation they played a hunch and got permission from the boy's parents to shave his head while the cameras rolled. The thick black hair was cut back until it was short and then, using a razor, they shaved the boy's left temple. There, for all to see, was a birth mark, but no ordinary birthmark - it was a birthmark in the shape of a bullet wound. In fact, when compared side by side with the autopsy photographs, the similarity to the husband's bullet wound was uncanny; more than that, they were identical even down to the powder burn displacement.

I remember clearly when I saw the birthmark come into view, amidst the tumbling hair, a shiver ran up my spine and still does every time I recall the episode. Is this proof or reincarnation? I don't know - there is always doubt. Would I believe in reincarnation now, if I had been part of the investigative team and checked that the hair wasn't a wig and the birthmark make-up? Almost certainly. I suppose I am always trying to build bridges to avoid the leap of faith, but without the leap it is no longer faith but science.

I enjoyed my recent discussion about Descartes with Hannah; she is extremely bright and gave me a great deal to think about. I am not sure if our paths have crossed before or whether there is just a great deal of empathy between us. There is definitely something there, but it could be just pheromones speaking to me. Just an old fart dreaming that a young woman could see anything else in him but a father figure. Part of me doesn't want this project to end, for Hannah to disappear from my life - this one.

The road demands my attention. I have left behind the urban landscape and am now driving alongside Cameron Lake. I can see a disused railway track clinging to the side of the steep hillside on the far shore and glimpse an occasional trestle bridge. Crossing these feats of engineering by train, and looking out at this glacier-fed lake, must have been breathtaking in more ways than one.

A mile or so on, at Cathedral Grove, I stop for a few minutes to stretch my legs. If ever there was a place for me to start my spiritual reawakening it is here, as I stand surrounded by 800-year-old Douglas-firs. It is a humbling experience to reach out and touch, even hug, a tree that was already fifteen years old when the Magna Carta was signed, and several metres high during the time of Ghengis Khan and Marco Polo. I began to think about our place in time. We live longer than we have ever lived before: eighty is a good age, ninety-plus is venerable, and yet the tree I am communing with was already one hundred years old when the Ottoman Empire was founded and the Plague swept through Europe. It was nearly 600 years old by the time Captain James Cook, the first European to land on these shores, arrived in 1778. I read an interpretive sign about my 'soul mate across time' and discover it is 76 metres tall and over nine metres in circumference. If only it could talk - what tales would it tell, what tears would it shed?

Back on the road I think of Desirée, ah Desirée, my mystical guide. I still don't know if you were real when you visited me in my bedroom in Budapest. But you are real now. You are part of my story; you have joined the list of players and have staked your claim as one who has influenced the outcome of the many journeys that have been undertaken. I wonder whether I need to believe in you, whether at some level I have to accept the influence you have had on me and on the outcome of the book, and on my belief in the QXCI. If Bill had a twin sister she would be just like Desirée.

I could see them having such great discussions and arguments, mirror images of each other - ying and yang. Desirée looking at Bill's waistline and tut-tutting, fussing over what he looked like, concerned for his well-being. She would be such an asset in his work with the QXCI, providing a female perspective and understanding of feminine health issues and emotions. Working side by side they could achieve so much. I start to second guess myself and consider that she might exist somehow on some level. She is a mystery, a paradox and, I believe, or rather feel, she is a catalyst for reaching the truth about so many things.

I am approaching Port Alberni, a mill town of 28,000 people, which is my favorite rest stop on the drive west to Tofino. Its effect on me differs, depending on the weather, and you never know what it's going to be like until a few minutes before you reach it. The sun can be offering its dappled warmth through the leaves of the ancient firs at Cathedral Grove and then, just the other side of the Port Alberni Hump, you can descend into thick fog and gloom of a type only the West Coast of Vancouver Island can lay on for you. Today I am lucky though - Port Alberni is bathed in spring sunshine.

I decide to stop at a coffee shop at the new and quite hip Alberni harbor Quay, an eclectic mix of galleries, gift shops and eateries. A Siberian husky comes to greet me as I start to drink my latté at one of the outside tables. We exchange a greeting well known to dog-lovers - me down on my knees, hands either side of his great, thick, furry neck ruffling through his fur, he looking at me disconcertingly with one blue and one brown eye, accepting the attention, as is his due.

Professor Nelson, Bill, unnerved me, even before I met him. When I met him for real it did nothing to assuage the feeling. He is so self-assured, so convinced that he is correct about everything, that he comes across at first as aggressively arrogant. Then one day I remembered something that Noel Coward said: "I cannot possibly be conceited, because I am perfect."

For the longest time I didn't know whether he was for real, and then I realized it didn't matter. Genius comes in all shapes and sizes and Bill was chameleon-like in his ability to adopt different personas, all the while displaying an ability to puncture the air with his ideas like a construction worker with a nail gun. He altered my perception of what people need to be in order to have an effect on the world on a grand scale. The world should be grateful that Professor Bill Nelson's mission on earth is to do good, because if it were otherwise then heaven forbid what the result might be.

I knew I would not feel his full influence on me for quite some time, but that when I did feel it, it would be of an unprecedented magnitude. The question was how would this influence manifest itself? The one thing I am sure of is that the next time we meet it will be very different. I have had an opportunity to reflect on the man and his invention and have a greater understanding of what makes him tick. My first meeting was overwhelming and I have to admit to being overly suspicious of the man and his motives. I felt uncomfortable and out of my depth to an extent I had not felt before. The man is still an enigma, but one that I am comfortable exploring.

When I was in Budapest I never really had an opportunity to find out more about his movie making or indeed watch any of his films, although I did tour his film studio. He is passionate about making documentaries that expose the sham that is the pharmaceutical industry. He has also made a film about the real Dracula, as opposed to the Hollywood version. From film producer to healthcare saviour - there is a lot more to Professor William Nelson than meets the eye.

If ever I get the chance to write his biography I know it will be a wild ride, but one that I am now mentally prepared for. The story will be worthy of a Hollywood movie or a BBC documentary, and both would be equally entertaining, shocking and controversial. I can't wait!

Once more the road demands my attention, or rather the scenery does. I leave civilization behind and head into wilderness. Shortly after Port Alberni I pass Sproat Lake where the last two surviving Mars water bombers have their home. It is fitting, I think, that creatures such as this, defying extinction, exist hidden away. These huge camels of the air, with a wingspan of 61 metres, swoop down on unsuspecting stretches of water and suck up more than 27 tonnes of it at a time, then drop it on errant forest fires across British Columbia and all over the world.

As I leave Sproat Lake behind, the last vestiges of civilization disappear: no more isolated houses, just the road remains as a final link to another world and to my past. The road itself is new. Until 1959 there was no road to Tofino at all and the only way in and out of the remote village was by boat - an arduous journey.

I can understand why people cut themselves off and live in remote communities; it is a form of escape from the rest of humanity's inhumanity. It never ceases to amaze me how anti-social people are. I am not referring to those that hide themselves away in places like the Tofino of 50 years ago, but to those that live cheek-by-jowl in towns and cities, but have little or no respect for each other. The people that drop litter, park in handicapped parking places, drink and drive, sell drugs to children and do the hundreds of other things that show a careless disregard of others. Pure selfishness exists and people try to escape from it, but eventually the world catches up with them or they miss being connected to it. Even with all its faults they give into this desire, or need for connectivity, and request, sometimes even demand, a link back to the world they tried to escape from. Even when a road was carved through the countryside it was, for the longest time, no more than stone chip. And this was before the days of Yuppie SUVs when the journey was a real adventure. Not that my journey isn't an adventure; I have no idea what I will confront except that I suspect there will be some demons to face.

The sky is bigger out here and the water clearer in the rushing springs that follow the road. I stop and venture down to the water's edge and hunch down on slippery rocks to splash water on my face. A few minutes earlier I had been dozing off and the nearside wheels of my car had wandered from the pavement, juddering me awake and announcing it was time to stop. As I look down into the water I can see freshwater crayfish hiding among the rocks, a little further upstream a Bald eagle perches at the very top of a spruce tree and I start to shed the urban skin that covers my psyche. I stop all movement, and listen, and then I hold my breath and the silence envelops me like a velvet cloak, comfortable and warm. Then the sounds of silence start to permeate the quiet and I begin to hear things that are usually hidden behind collateral noise. The spring has its own sound as it travels to the sea and then, as the eagle takes off, I can hear the displacement of air from its mighty wings. I wander back to the car. It is out of place here, but I feel less so than a few minutes ago.

Back on the road the landscape becomes even more entrancing as the road starts to climb. I have passed brackish lakes punctured with the stumps of trees, which look like so many prehistoric creatures rising from the deep, and pristine rivers flowing over grey rock worn smooth with the passage of time. Now I have reached a summit of sorts and as the road takes a sharp turn to the left, I am on the edge. There is a drop of several hundred feet on my right. Below, the sea, as it flows inland for several miles along an estuary, is a deep blue. It gives the feeling of great depth and intent: there is purpose here. Trees hide the view from me and I am heading down toward the junction where travellers have to decide whether to turn left for Ucluelet or right for Tofino. As I approach the junction, I have no hesitation in turning right. I know my destination geographically, if not spiritually, although in this case they may be one and the same.

The boundary of the Pacific Rim National Park is just a few miles further on and I start to keep a watchful eye out for black bears foraging for berries on the roadside, a common sight on this stretch of road. I never cease to be amazed when I see a bear in the wild. I've seen hundreds in zoos over the years, but they are just shadows of the real thing; they have no spirit - their history is one of bricks and mortar and not of wild fruit and temperate rain forest.

It is not surprising that many people feel a spiritual awakening when they visit the Esowista peninsula and the town of Tofino, which sits like a jewel at its northernmost tip. There is evidence that man has lived on this coast for at least 4,300 years, and the oral history of the Nuu-chah-nulth nation lays claim to the fact that they have inhabited the area since the world was created.

The period before the European settlers arrived were good years for the indigenous population. They were rich in comparison with other native groups in North America. The sea and the forest were good to them and provided an abundance of resources such as food, shelter and clothing. Their connection to the land was a spiritual one - they co-existed with Mother Earth and the bond was powerful. Society was strong, their culture complex. And then the white man came - at first explorers and traders, then settlers. With them came disease. The natives had no defense against this silent germ warfare. Smallpox, tuberculosis, dysentery and measles all took their toll. It took less than one hundred years to see the native population decimated by up to ninety percent.

A few miles from Tofino I turn left down a dirt track, the dust billowing out from behind the car like the after effect of an explosion, following and threatening to engulf me. I have been here before with Steve, my young researcher friend. The cabin was built by his grandfather sixty years ago as a home for his new wife, who travelled from Finland to start a new life on the Pacific coast with him. Over the years it has been renovated and modernized. It even has electricity now, but it has never lost its rustic pioneer charm. I love the cabin and sometimes dream of buying a place just like it. You don't so much live on this coast as experience it. The winter storms are ferocious, and the mist can envelop the coast for days on end. You have to learn to endure the many shades of grey and the cold biting rain that attacks your face from a multiplicity of angles. But then, you have days when the sky is so blue it almost hurts your eyes. There are moments when you look out to sea and a whale breeches or spy-hops, checking you out curiously, and mornings when the mist hangs on the cliffs and crags in a hundred shades of purple, mauve and a unique greyish blue that I have only ever seen on the West Coast of Canada.

I open the door of the cabin and it is just as I remember it. The smell of wood smoke from sixty long winters permeates the interior and launches an attack on the nostalgia receptors in my brain. The stove is original, and I know if I try really hard I will be able to see Steve's grandfather, Tuukka, fussing over it, encouraging it to give its all and keep them warm.

I quickly unpack and hang my clothes in the rough hewn closet made from a single tree felled by Tuukka in the late 1940s. Once I have staked my claim to my temporary homestead, I feel secure enough to venture out onto the deck and take in a view that never ceases to have the power to calm me to the core of my being. Pine trees overhang the deck and frame the scene. I am looking out at the Pacific Ocean - I once read a book called the Commanding Sea and remember the awe the author had for the ocean. To my mind, there is no more commanding sea than the one I am looking at this very moment. By now the sun is low in the sky and the tide is out and the sand is a burnished gold.

I was here once in late January during storm season, a time when gale after gale smashes into the shore and the waves are as high as houses. Something called the Aleutian Low builds in the Gulf of Alaska and then moves southward. Vancouver Island is right in the path of the storm track and the drama unfolds. Tourists come from all over the world to experience this demonstration of Mother Nature's power. Some of them challenge it with disastrous effect. They walk out onto slippery rocks jutting out into the angry sea, the waves crashing all around them and then, without warning, a rogue wave plucks them off the shore as easily and quickly as a toad snaps a fly from the air. Some survive to tell the tale, but others will never defy her superiority again.

What surprises me is that I find this place just as spiritual, just as uplifting, and at the same time just as calming, anytime of the year. Its spirituality is not bound exclusively to the geography, the weather, it's history or its link to the sacred past of its earliest inhabitants: it is the connection one feels to all these things. I am sure other people come here and just experience the splendor of its landscape, walk the beaches and commune with nature, and never make the link to its mystic plane.

The weather here is often harsh and even in spring and summer it can be inclement to say the least, but it never bothers me as it does back in Victoria. I can cope better here. I can deal with my feelings and gain a better perspective on my life. Despair has no meaning here for me; everything is ordered and the competitiveness that runs my life at home does not exist here - it is like a loaded gun I check at the door when I arrive. I sometimes wonder what drags me back to my workaday existence time and time again. I suppose it is a fear that if I stay too long all those things will creep into my life here, and then what? Where would I go to find my brief respites?

The sun is lower now and the colors are from a different palette. A few clouds on the horizon are standing out in sharp contrast to the sky behind them, which has turned from gold to red to the muted and intermingled colors of a Turner seascape. The clouds are being stretched out by some unseen hand along the horizon, changing from dark grey through to a hodgepodge of blue-grays and grey-purples, their edges polished by the setting sun.

"I thought I'd find you here."

"Hannah! What the devil are you doing here - how did you know where I'd be?"

"When I spoke to you last night I knew you were down, really down - I was worried. Your neighbor said that you packed up the car and left early, so I called your wife and she said you were going to Tofino to finish the book."

"Well Sherlock, I came up for some peace and quiet, to see if I could get my head around a few things."

The truth was, I was pleased to see her. She has been such an important part of my life lately. The events of the last eighteen months have been tough for me. I have had to come to terms with a lot of personal fears, one of them being a fear of belief. Some things have become clearer though, especially my view of myself. I am beginning to understand who I am and, through recognition, has come a change in my personality and in my core being. My comfortable marriage is just that - it is a convenience, for both Suzie and me. It's not really a marriage at all; we have become room mates, drifting apart into easy coexistence.

"Simon, crank up the barbecue, I bought some salmon steaks with me."

Being with Hannah is easy; it is comfortable, but not in the same way as it is with Suzie. With Suzie we each do our own thing, keep out of each other's way and it works fine, to a point. With Hannah I experience harmony, she is ying to my yang, and the comfort comes from knowing implicitly how each other feels, and from being able to relate to each other on a higher plane. I thought again about whether we might have spent time together in another life.

I prepared a salad while Hannah rummaged through cupboards to see what she could use to concoct a dressing. "How close are you to finishing the book?" she asked, standing on a chair with her head half way into one of the top cupboards.

"Pretty close," I answered. "I have a few loose ends to pull together and I need an ending. I'm just not sure whether I can wholeheartedly endorse the device."

"But Simon, after all the research I've done, all the patients and practitioners I've interviewed, how could you not believe?"

"I know, I know. There's plenty of evidence, but you know I have difficulty with belief issues. If only the medical world in general endorsed it."

"If they did you wouldn't be writing a book on it. Professor Nelson would be pictured on the front page of Time magazine receiving a Nobel Prize, where he belongs. The whole world would be writing about him."

I thought about this for a few seconds and found myself wanting to believe, wanting desperately to cross over to the other side. I looked at Hannah as she added the ingredients she had found to a small cracked china bowl. I felt an overwhelming feeling of well-being sweep over me and an urgent desire to hold her in my arms.

"So much has happened, so much synergy in the events that have led to us here. So many coincidences, so much growth. I feel that fate has brought me to this point and that I am close to finding an answer, perhaps more than one."

"Simon, I have watched your metaphysical struggle for the last year. I've seen you come to terms with your personal fears and I've seen you struggle with the structure of belief. I believe your journey is almost over. The book is a catalyst for a life change for you; it will take you to the next stage of your journey, not just through this life, but in your total existence. You know you really believe in reincarnation, you just won't let yourself admit it. You know you really believe in the QXCI, but you still can't quite make that leap of faith. That's why you came here - to sacrifice your agnosticism in a place where you feel, deep down, the spirituality you have not been able to allow into your life. I came because I feel I had to be part of this experience, that I was always part of it, that somehow I was responsible for you losing your faith in the first place. Not in this life perhaps, but I know it is important I'm here with you at this time, in this life."

"That was quite the speech, and I agree that you belong here, that whatever is going to happen needs both of us. Dr. Voll, all those years ago promised so much from energetic medicine and I know... I think I know, that the QXCI is that promise fulfilled. But I still need that sign. I still feel like I did in that church all those years ago, desperately wanting to believe, but something in my brain is still holding out for some sort of sign."

We lapsed into a comfortable silence while I cooked the salmon. At one point I looked down to the water's edge, the tide was a long way out. I saw a figure paddling in the cold water, his pants rolled up to just beneath his knees. "Look Hannah, see that guy down there wading?"

She leaned right and left to look round a branch that obstructed her view, "Yeh, so what?"

"He looks so much like Bill."

"You mean Professor Nelson. How can you tell from this far away?"

"I don't know, it just looks like him. It must be my mind playing tricks. This book seems to be taking me over; it's all I can think off." At that moment the stranger looked up toward the cabin, and although I couldn't make out his face, a chill ran up my spine. By the time I turned around Hannah was back in the kitchen gathering cutlery and cutting a French loaf and arranging it in a basket she had discovered while rummaging through the cupboards.

We ate outside under a canopy of stars and after dinner we sat on the deck on a rickety old bench. For the longest time we sat and listened to the waves until the air cooled enough for me to be able to feel the warmth of her body. The stars and the moon played with the waves and gave us a slow romantic waltz of light. Hannah reached across the few inches that separated us and stroked my hand. I have never felt so in need of comfort and understanding. I was at a crossroads, or more accurately, a precipice in my life. I was beginning to feel that whatever was going to happen was out of my control and for the first time that seemed all right. Hannah stood up without letting go of my hand and drew me up next to her. She affected a slow and practiced flick of her head so that there was a flash of long blond hair, and then she kissed me so lightly, so gently, that I could almost have mistaken it for the gentle breeze off the ocean.

It is five in the morning and my life has changed irrevocably. I have been lying here for the last fifteen minutes listening to the peaceful breathing of Hannah beside me. I dare not look across for fear that I will discover this is all a dream and that I am really here by myself in Tuukka's cabin. I summon my courage and turn my head and there she is. I can't believe that we slept together last night; she is so young, so beautiful and so important to me. I want to hold her tight, so tight she won't be able to get away, ever. But I am afraid that if I do the spell will be broken and I will just be a tired, middle-aged man suffering from delusional fantasies. There I go again, struggling with belief.

I decide to go for a walk, clear my head, make sense of what has transpired over the last few hours and over the last year. I feel close to being able to resolve the book and also my ongoing metaphysical struggle, very close.

There is an early morning mist and the air is fresh. Flocks of birds occupy the low water line, sandpipers perhaps, busy with breakfast. At the far end of the beach there is a jagged point with mist hanging to its lower reaches. Right at the point it looks as if there is a man sitting in a deckchair looking out to sea. It takes me a few minutes to realize that at this distance it must be very large, a rock formation, not a man. Pity. The thought of a sentinel watching the sea like some ancient mythical god would be fitting for this place. But what would he be looking out for, I wonder.

There is no one else on the beach, and the sea is unusually quite. I hear a soft whooshing sound above me and I look up to see an osprey flying no more than fifteen feet above my head. It is a beautiful bird and from below it looks white with barred undersides to its wings. The osprey resembles other eagles but is the sole member of the family Pandionidae. It is one of a kind, like just like the QXCI, which may resemble other devices but belongs to its own genus entirely.

Now that Hannah is here I feel ready to write the final chapter of the book. The evidence is overwhelmingly positive: Hannah did a great job in researching, tracking down and interviewing so many witnesses. And, if I expected the practitioners to all be kooks practicing their own kind of twenty-first century magic, I was wrong.

Penny, a sensible, articulate woman devoted to her clients, under-played the enormity of what the QXCI could achieve. She was modesty personified, in terms of her own abilities and those of the machine. Her matter-of-fact approach made her all the more believable. Leslie, a totally professional practitioner, runs her practice in a businesslike manner while helping so many people. Her enthusiasm for the device, and her excitement at meeting other QXCI practitioners and sharing her success stories, was contagious. Her willingness to push the boundaries and grow with the QXCI made her a pioneer. And all the others: Ben with his fascination for the technology, Gerry with his explanation of how the device becomes one with the patient and adapts to change, and Marie reminding us that the device can tune our three natures - body, mind and spirit. At this moment in time I am working hard on mind and spirit, when I get back home I will book an appoint-ment and allow the QXCI to bring my body into line.

Most surprising of all were the case studies Hannah discovered. I appreciated the way she kept away from the more miraculous sto-ries, although there were plenty and they were all absolutely con-vincing. The stories she suggested I use were of ordinary people, struggling through ordinary illnesses that were devastating their lives. They offered testimony enough to the work of the QXCI and the practitioners in the frontline of this new era of healthcare. One thing I am sure of is that one day there will be a QXCI unit in every home, and practitioners and doctors around the world will be linked to patients via the Internet.

The mist is starting to lift a little as I walk farther from the cabin. Steve's research on the pharmaceutical companies showed that money can bring trust, even where it is not earned or deserved. Professor Nelson's device would be commonplace in doctor's offices by now if it were owned by a major pharma. So where does the truth lay? In the mouths of those with the most money, or those for whom money is a secondary issue.

All I know is that if the QXCI was widely available there would be more people with wonderful stories of renewed health and less people suffering from the side effects of drugs and invasive medical procedures.

Perhaps I don't need to believe in a God; perhaps I just need to believe. The beach is strewn with logs washed ashore, victims of the storms, washed white and smooth. I choose one and sit looking out to sea. The waves are a little higher than last night, but still benign. Wispy clouds stretch across the horizon catching the early morning sun long before it will reach me sitting here with a forest of tall pines behind me.

Once again I feel the spirituality of this place, its sanctity. Back to square one. It's just like sitting in the church all over again - I'm still waiting for a sign. Perhaps it is impossible for me to believe with all of my heart, to make the leap of faith and just believe in myself, my place in the universe, my purpose, in the quantum magic of the QXCI.

The beach is quiet, even the birds are savoring the gradual warmth of the rising sun. And then I feel a hand on my shoulder, barely touching me, just a presence. For some reason I am not surprised, or at least not shocked. I have no fear and no sudden urge to jump up, turn around and fight or run. I half expect to see Hannah standing there, or perhaps it isn't a hand at all, not a flesh and blood one at least. Then I catch a scent that is out of place here, mixing with the salt, sea and seaweed smell of the beach. The last time I smelled it was in Budapest - it is the unmistakable perfume, Chanel No. 5. Slowly I turn my head. Desirée is smiling down on me. I hear Hannah calling me from down the beach and wave at her. I turn back to Desirée but she is gone.

"What are you doing out here darling?" Hannah said breathlessly.

"Learning to believe, and realizing that even if I haven't found my God yet, I already have a guardian angel. And so does the rest of the world."

Acknowledgements

Firstly, I would like to thank my wonderful wife Sheila and my sons, Adam and Joshua, for supporting me over the last eighteen months and for putting up with my long absences when I was holed up in my study researching and writing this book.

My sincere thanks to Jilly Margo who carried out much of the research and all of the practitioner and patient interviews. The character of Hannah developed and took on a life of its own because of your input, and the book is all the better for it.

Mary-Louise Leidl took my words and edited them; tirelessly correcting the thousands of typos, punctuation errors and grammatical howlers. She also helped tremendously in renaming the chapters. Thank you.

Lilo Binakaj for his endless patience and commitment to excellence in the design of the jacket, the page layout and for making me look at least passable in the photographs.

Karen and Ryan Williams from Quantum Life were my staunchest supporters and gave me the confidence to carry on. Thank you for your support and friendship.

To Professor William Nelson (Bill): this book is a tribute to your genius. It was a privilege to meet you. I look back at my time with you in Budapest as a turning point in my life. I hope to meet you again soon.

Finally, I would like to thank the unsung heroes of this book: the practitioners who use the QXCI every day and the patients who have been helped by it. You know who you are, this is your story.

Thank-you,

Michael P Wicks (September 2002)
Your Corporate Writer
email: mike@yourcorporatewriter.com

QUANTUM LIFE

Quantum Life LLC is an internationally registered broker for the QXCI Quantum Xrroid Consciousness Interface Software System with agents and distributors worldwide. Spurred on by personal tragedies with the public health system the owners of Quantum Life recognize the need for better health care and that a fundamental shift in consciousness is needed on this planet.

Traditional "dis-ease" care creates a vicious circle with no emphasis placed on lifestyle management and preventative health care.

Bio-energetic medicine has opened the door to a philosophy of health care that was used thousands of years ago. Tapping into these resources and understanding ancient philosophies, then combining this with modern technology is creating a paradigm shift in the way we view medicine today.

Computers are already used extensively throughout the mainstream medical system. It is only a matter of time before we will be able to view the human body in "real time" Realizing the body is dynamic, and in a constant state of flux, the

QXCI is now able to track these changes and offer corrective therapies. This is truly 21st century medicine.

Quantum Life is committed to furthering knowledge and understanding of the fantastic benefits of bio energetic medicine. Based in Santa Barbara, Quantum Life LLC runs regular seminars throughout the world educating people how to use this new technology. As a software-based consulting company Quantum Life LLC is dedicated to bringing this technology to people of all walks of life.

For further information on this technology please contact:

Quantum Life LLC
2022 Cliff Drive
Santa Barbara CA
93109 USA

Email:info@quantum-life.com
www.quantum-life.com
Tel: 1 (866) 869-0278